Roddick

WALL STREET JOURNAL & USA TODAY
BESTSELLING AUTHOR
KB WINTERS

Copyright and Disclaimer

This book is a work of fiction. The names, characters, places and incidents are products of the writer's imagination and have been used fictitiously and are not to be construed as real. Any resemblance to persons, living or dead, actual events, locales or organizations is entirely coincidental.

Copyright © 2017 BookBoyfriends Publishing

All rights reserved. No part of this publication may be reproduced, stored in or introduced into a retrieval system, or transmitted, in any form, or by any means (electronic, mechanical, photocopying, recording, or otherwise) without the prior written permission of the copyright owner. The author acknowledges the trademarked status and trademark owners of various products referenced in this work of fiction, which have been used without permission. The publication/use of the trademarks is not authorized, associated with, or sponsored by the trademark owners.

RODDICK

CAOS MC Book 3

By KB Winters

Prologue

Roddick

"What the hell am I doing here?" I knew it was pointless to ask the question since I was clearly inside an interrogation room with one of those mirrors we're supposed to pretend doesn't have a shit ton of agents on the other side of it, uncomfortable metal chairs, and even the fucking swinging light bulb overhead. I was sitting inside a fucking stereotype. But I asked anyway because I hadn't done shit wrong. "If you don't have shit to say, I'm requesting a lawyer and invoking my right to remain silent." Assholes thought they could bully me, but they would soon learn I was no chump.

The door finally opened and two suits walked in to the dimly lit room, the yellow tinged bulb flickering. Suit number one was a chick with red hair pulled into a ponytail, big green eyes, and freckles that made her look all of fifteen. The other dude might as well have been Captain fucking America with his slicked back blond hair and sharp blue eyes. They both wore ill-fitting suits that marked them as government agents rather than corporate types. "You're in no position to make demands," the redhead said.

I stared at her as though she hadn't said a word. I was off fighting for Uncle Sam before she was even born, and I didn't intimidate easily. Too bad for her. "Am I leaving, or is somebody gonna tell me what the fuck I'm doing here?"

The man took the seat across from me and pulled out a manila folder, a move I'd seen more than a few cops make over the years. In the movies. "I'm Agent Jack Brockton and that's Molly Johnson. We're part of a new task force assembled to deal with the cartels." He laid out several photos of a truck burning in the desert. "This truck was found just outside of San Diego. Inside we found twenty people, still being identified. We're pretty sure this truck belongs to the Mexican Devils."

RODDICK

It wouldn't surprise me if it did. The cartel's main business was drugs, mostly heroin, but they also had houses of girls and women all over the country. "What does this have to do with me? I'm doing my part to keep this shit from crossing the border, you Feds are the ones falling down on the job." Arms crossed, I waited for them to deny it and pretend they gave a damn.

Agent Pollyanna, I meant Molly, leaned forward with what was supposed to be a scowl on her face. "You're not exactly on the right side of the law, are you?"

I leaned back and gave her my most charming grin. "If that was true, sweetheart, you'd have me in bracelets and trying to leverage some type of compromise, so cut the shit and tell me what you want." I could tell she didn't like my tone, but I didn't give a damn. I didn't like her tone either.

Brockton laughed and leaned back, kicking up his feet and crossing them at the ankles. He laid out photos of two more trucks burned to a crisp and photos of CAOS carrying Minx from that warehouse while some Devils took care of the trash that used to belong to our club, Wagman and Rocky. "We know what your club has been up to which is why we leave you alone. But now we need you boys to help us out, because this shit has gotten too big."

"I'm listening." Captain America was right about one thing, the Mexican Devils had been sending more drugs into the U.S. and more people into Mexico.

"We need your club to start taking shipments of drugs from the cartel so we can trace the drugs, but more importantly, we need to trace the cash. See where it turns up."

I heard what he wasn't saying loud and clear. "You think Lazarus has a boss." Cash thought the same thing after meeting Lazarus, but I'd keep that info to myself. For now.

Agent Johnson sighed and got in my face. Again. "Don't worry about what we think."

"Call off your girl, Brockton." She was seriously testing my patience with her Chihuahua routine. I didn't believe in punching women, but this was no woman—she was a cop—a cop getting on my last nerve.

"We do," Brockton answered, hardly sparing her a glance. "But we don't know who it is, so we need to see where the money ends up. That's where you come in."

"And the club will be immune from anything done to help your task force?"

"Yep."

"Maybe," answered Pollyanna.

I stood and towered over the fiery redhead. "If that's the case, I'll take my chance with whatever dirt you think you have on me and my club." I didn't need this shit seeing as my guys were doing what the fucking Feds should be doing in the first place. "Good luck."

"Wait!" Brockton stood and glared at Johnson before turning back to me. "Full immunity. Just do some deals and get us what we need."

"I need to talk to the club first but yeah, okay." Brockton held out his hand, and I took it. Dealing with him would be easier than the girl because guys like Brockton shot straight and only cared about getting the bad guys. "Get the paperwork drawn up. You'll hear from me soon."

"Make us wait too long and we'll find a reason to do this with handcuffs." Johnson was a real ballbuster but not even in a good way. One of those women who thought acting like a man was the best way. She probably had a set of cojones under that suit.

"Try it and I'll tip off Lazarus." With a whistle, I walked away.

Chapter One

Cherie

It wasn't even midnight yet and the ER was already a madhouse—no, it was at least three steps up from a madhouse. And the worst part? It was only Thursday which meant it was too damn early for all the craziness. My shift started at ten since we were on twelve hour shifts to accommodate the fact that we were the only hospital around after two others had closed in the past decade. Already four gunshot wounds had come in from Ojo, a few drunks and a junkie who'd OD'd, most of whom we'd been able to save.

I had just finished stitching up the eyebrow of a woman whose boyfriend didn't like the way she fried his chicken when another call came in. Domestic violence cases made up a bulk of my work as an ER nurse, and I hated it. But what I hated more was seeing the same women time and again who couldn't stand up to their abusers and worse, who wouldn't leave them. Those cases left me exhausted both mentally and physically, so as soon as I discharged her, I made my way to my favorite dark corner of the cafeteria with a salad and a cheeseburger. I knew this meal could end at any moment, it was the nature of ER work, so I ate fast while looking over job postings online.

It was time for me to leave Brently for good. Too much crap was going on in town and my brother Baz, along with his club, CAOS, were always in the middle of it. They weren't bad guys, they were all veterans with massive hero complexes which meant they often found themselves playing the good guys to the worst bad guys of the world. So far Talon, the club's Vice President's new wife, had been assaulted and Minx, fiancée of the club Secretary, Cash, had been kidnapped and beaten badly. As Baz's sister, I knew my luck wouldn't hold out much longer so I worked hard, picking up as many extra shifts as I could to pay the hospital back for my RN degree.

Then, I'd be gone.

RODDICK

I tapped a job posting in Minnesota, ignoring the stinging in my chest as I thought about our mother. She was from St. Paul. Had grown up there and fled after the death of her twin brother. She'd left us not long after our dad died, leaving me all alone while nineteen-year-old Baz was in the Army. My brother's friend, Torch, stepped in to care for me, a ten-year-old girl who'd been abandoned. I scratched that idea right away, Minnesota was off the table. Permanently.

I'd just taken the final bite of my burger when I was summoned to the ER for an EDP, because emotionally disturbed people were now my area of expertise. I trashed my food and put the tray on top, wiping my hands on my scrubs and shoving my phone into my hip pocket. "What do we have?" I asked as soon as I entered the exam room, but no answer could be heard over her shouting.

"They're burning! You have to save them or they will all die!"

I walked over to her with a serene expression on my face and a calming voice that would settle her. "Who is burning, miss?"

"*Los bebes! Las chicas!* They are burning."

The babies. The girls. I had a feeling she was more than a junkie, so I gave her half a dose of sedative hoping to get her more coherent. "I need you to calm down, ma'am, so I can treat your wounds." She had burns, scratches, and cuts all over her body, but the soles of her feet and her hands seemed to have taken the brunt of the damage. "*Calma por favor.*"

Big brown eyes looked up at me and nodded. "*Gracias.*"

I smiled and got to work cleaning and bandaging her as the sedative kicked in and her breathing evened out, her heart rate returned to normal. "Now that you're calm, perhaps you can tell me your name?"

"Monica."

"Okay, Monica, can you tell me what happened to you?"

RODDICK

She looked terrified, and I swallowed the ball of fear that settled in my stomach. "They put us in a truck headed for the border," she began in heavily accented English. "But something happened and it stopped. Then fire. Everywhere. We were trapped. I got out, and I ran. They will be coming for me."

Before I could ask another question, she drifted off to sleep, which I was sure she needed after what she'd been through. I made a note in her chart to alert me when she woke up and went to take care of a double whammy, a junkie with a split lip, a swollen eye, and a cut wrist.

Fuck my life.

After dealing with that particular mess, I needed a breather and a change of clothes. I headed out to my car, scanning the parking lot because two in the morning was not a good time to be out alone. "Shit." Two of my tires were flat, and though I knew the odds were slim it was just misfortune. I ignored the sliver of unease and texted my brother for a ride before reaching inside for my bag.

A pair of hands grabbed me from behind and slammed me against the trunk of my car. "Tell that *puta* to keep her fucking mouth shut or she'll end up like the others."

I closed my eyes and swallowed back the lump of fear that strangled my throat. I steadied my nerves and took note of what I could. Spanish accent. Short, probably five-six to my five-four, young based on the pitch of his voice. Kind of chubby. "You'll have to be more specific. Which *puta*?" Even though I was terrified, I steeled my voice. It wasn't the first time an angry boyfriend or husband showed up to threaten the staff.

"Get your fucking hands off her!" an enraged voice shouted from behind us, and I knew instantly who it was. A voice I'd heard many times growing up and now in my dreams as well. He pulled the man off of me, and I heard several blows before a groan of agony. "You okay, Cherie?"

I nodded and looked up into clear silver blue eyes, crinkled with worry at the corners. Those eyes

RODDICK

I've dreamed about looking at me with love since I was about thirteen-years-old. "Roddick? What are you doing here?"

"Are you okay?" he asked again, a little bit gruff and a little concerned.

I nodded again, taken off balance by his nearness, by the masculine scent I'd recognize anywhere. "I think so. I don't know who he is. But I have a feeling I know exactly who he wanted." I picked up my bag and started toward the hospital entrance. "Why are you here, anyway?"

"I was on my way here because Talon went into labor."

"She did?" I gasped and cupped my hand over my mouth, because he gently took my hand in his and squeezed. "She's fine, Cherie. I'm in my way up now."

"I'll come by Maternity and check on her when my shift is over." I looked away from his gaze, feeling a surge of emotions overcoming me. "Wait. Why are you out here in the employee lot?" I asked, confused.

He smirked and rubbed a hand over his five o'clock shadow. "I got a text from Baz saying you needed a ride so I came out here to see where you'd parked."

"Where is he?" My older brother apparently thought he could keep tabs on me while hiding his own life.

"Club business, sweetheart."

I raised an eyebrow. I hated that answer. The club used it for fucking everything.

"Chill, Cherie. He's loading up some bikes to take back east. He'll be gone for a few." I nodded and turned after grabbing my spare scrubs from the car. He walked beside me, his long, lazy strides made it look as though I was running just to keep up.

"What did that asshole want?"

"What?" I couldn't concentrate with Roddick so close. He distracted me, made me want to throw all my good sense out the window and ravish the man. But an experienced man two decades older than me wouldn't want anything to do with this shy virgin with her nose constantly stuck in a book.

"You said you didn't know who he was, but you obviously know what—or who—he wanted."

Damn, he'd caught all that? I shook my head because *of course* he did. Roddick had been a soldier and a damn good one based on Baz's estimation, some type of off the books operations leader. I never asked because I wasn't sure if I wanted to know. I told him about Monica and what she'd said to me. "That's it. I wasn't sure if she was half delirious, but I believed her. I guess it's a good thing I did."

"Shit!" His huge hands curved around my shoulders to bring me to a stop. "Don't come out here alone again. I'll meet you in the cafeteria when your shift is over." He winced, and instantly my hands went to his midsection.

I could have argued, but I didn't. As much as I hated his bossiness, I knew he wanted me safe. And I couldn't pass up a chance to spend more time with him. "Fine. Let me take a look at that wound and then I'll come up to see Talon when I get a chance."

"No need," he said quickly.

"Then I'll find my own way home. Good night."

He growled and reached for my arm, wincing again. "Fine. Let's go."

I smiled to myself at his gruff tone. The only other person I'd miss as much as my brother when I left Brently, was Roddick.

***

Roddick

A few days later, I'd spoke to Mick as soon as Talon and the brand new baby girl were home. "Mick, I know you'd rather be with Talon and baby Megan, but some shit is going down and I need you."

After what Cherie had told me, I knew the club had to help the task force. I gave Mick the rundown on what the agents wanted from the club, what Cherie had heard, and the burning bodies that kept turning up. "I hate to bring this to the table, Mick. What if the guys don't want to let it go after this shit is over?"

Mick nodded. I knew he'd get it. "We have to do it, man. Any one of those burned bodies could have easily been Minx."

"We have to do it anyway or else the Feds are gonna turn their attention to the club. Now, I don't want to just give in to all their demands." I'd been thinking about it for a while, and I knew what I had to do for CAOS. For Brently. "I don't want the whole club involved in this shit, Mick."

"I got it. Me, Cash, Dagger and Torch only."

We spent an hour outlining plans for how this would work, and how we'd deal with the aftermath. "Now go on home to your family and I'll touch base again soon." We said our goodbyes, and I pulled out my phone. "Meet at Jade Dragon in an hour and do me a favor, try not to look so much like a fucking fed, yeah?" I ended the call without another word. I hated fucking cops more than anything, but I needed to let

Sheriff Darlington know his town was in the eye of this shit storm.

After that stop, I went to Jade Dragon and ordered an appetizer platter so it wouldn't look suspicious if anyone saw us together. When Brockton arrived, he slid into the middle of the booth. "I'm glad you left your girlfriend at home."

"She's new. Overeager, but Johnson's all right."

"I don't trust her."

"You don't have to, because I do," he said with more feeling than I'd seen from him since our first meeting.

"It's your funeral. Now let's just get to it." I outlined my conditions for helping, and I could see he didn't like some of them, but I didn't give a shit. "We help you with this and the club gets the reward money on Lazarus' head. All of it."

"I can't guarantee that."

"You'll have to because if anyone finds out about this, we're all at risk. You have the protection of the government, we have wives, girlfriends, and children to protect."

Brockton sighed and ran a hand through his hair, shaking his head and muttering under his breath. "I'll have to clear it with the boss. Meet me at task force HQ on Monday." He took a final bite of the shumai and stood, grabbing the leather jacket that made him look less like Captain America.

"One more thing, Brockton." I'd told him about the woman in the ER, but I didn't give him her name. "Another truck was found outside Ojo, confirming her story."

"Shit!" He stepped outside and barked into the phone with more than a few 'fucks' and 'shits' thrown in for good measure. He walked back in a few minutes later. "Thanks for the intel, Roddick."

With Brockton gone, I sat in the booth, eating egg rolls and satay as I thought about my life. I'd been in CAOS since I was a young man, a soldier before that. At forty-four, I felt ancient compared to the prospects, hell even compared to Mick. I didn't even feel fucking young anymore. I didn't feel as strong and energetic as I once was, especially the long healing process after taking a fucking bullet. The violence only seemed to get worse no matter what the club did, and in such a filthy fucking world it would be harder and harder for CAOS to stay clean.

I looked over at an old couple enjoying the buffet as much as they enjoyed being together, and it made me think that maybe it was time I got a life outside of CAOS. Like a woman of my own and maybe some ankle biters.

Yeah right, like that shit would ever happen.

Chapter Two

Cherie

"Is Roddick here?" I had already searched the clubhouse bedrooms and even the apartment upstairs, and the man was nowhere to be found. "I'm supposed to meet him here."

"He's not here, but I can help you with whatever you need." A cute blond who couldn't be more than a few years older than me made a lewd move with his hips, flashing a dimpled smile my way.

"Dude, that's Baz's sister! You're dead." Track had been part of CAOS for a few years now, and he had that whole sexy biker thing going with long black hair and penetrating eyes that were nearly as black. "He's at home today. Said he wouldn't be in at all."

Well that was just fucking great. My shift at the hospital had just ended which meant I'd been up for going on sixteen hours with no sleep, and he couldn't even be bothered to show up. "Thanks, Track." I sent a wave as I made my way to the parking lot and away from the clubhouse. The stubborn man needed his bandages changed and more antibiotic cream from the bullet he'd taken almost two months ago. Despite his white knight routine in the parking lot the other night, he wasn't fully healed.

I pulled up to his house with the same amused grin I always wore, because he'd chosen a home in a family neighborhood where kids rode their bikes on the sidewalk and played kickball in the street. It was so normal it often made me wonder if I knew the real Roddick. Not that I knew him at all, actually. As far as he was concerned, I was just the annoying little kid who used to follow him everywhere with stars in her eyes. He'd seen me with pigtails and braces, and he'd been there when Baz taught me how to defend myself. How to shoot. But this neighborhood spoke of a man who wanted something more than what he had. More than what he'd chosen to have.

I walked up to the one and a half story California bungalow. It was blue with white trim and a neat lawn. I knocked and no one answered, so I dug around the birdfeeder for the spare key and pushed inside, hoping I wasn't about to find something I wouldn't be able to forget. "Roddick?" He wasn't in any of the common areas, so I kept going. "Rod? Roddick, are you here?" Oh, he was here all right. On his back with one arm slung over his face, sheet riding so low on his waist that one small tug would give me my first look at him. I licked my lips at the sight he made.

Despite his age he was in fantastic shape, body hard though not as defined as his younger years. A prominent vee could still be seen behind the sprinkling of chocolate hair that disappeared under the sheet. Damn, he was far more manly, more built than in my dreams. Then I saw it, blood seeping through the bandage, and clenched my teeth. *Get it together, girl.* I couldn't just stand there ogling a sleeping man. I needed to look under that bandage, and he'd been putting me off for a few days. I turned and left the bedroom, heading to the kitchen where I made a pot of coffee, cleaned up, and made some food. I knew I shouldn't take care of him like that, but

I wanted to, and I had to wait for him to wake up so I kept busy.

But even that could only last so long.

I set the rustic pot pie in the oven to stay warm and went to check on him again, this time noticing that he felt a bit warmer than normal. A light sheen of sweat covered his face and chest. "Shit." A gasp escaped when his hand wrapped around my wrist, keeping it pressed to the warmth of his chest muscles, twisting so I was on my back underneath him.

"Cherie babe, if you wanted into my bed all you had to do was say so." He laughed and his blue eyes glittered, making me forget why I'd shown up in the first place. At least temporarily.

He was so big, so male. So hot and strong pressed up against me. And the man wore nothing but a pair of boxers. Loose boxers that let me feel everything. And it was significant. My body began to respond to his nearness, heart racing, breathing shallow, and my body grew warm with desire. I squirmed to get him to move, but he groaned and flexed his hips, making me gasp. "I didn't come here to get in your bed."

But I don't mind staying, just for a little while.

"Keep telling yourself that." He leaned in close, and I swore he sniffed my hair, but I was too busy inhaling his scent to notice. Finally, he rolled away, and I felt a wave of disappointment. "Why else did you come, then?"

I blew out a breath that might have been annoyance, but probably more toward sexual frustration. "Bullet hole in your body ringing any bells?"

"Now that you mention it." He rolled onto his back with a groan, stretching out and giving me the most delicious view of his body. The little devil on my shoulder told me to drag my tongue across every inch of his skin and to linger on the tattoos that had enchanted me for years, before stripping naked and begging him to take me. But the angel reminded me that I couldn't handle a man like Roddick. *If* he wanted me for real. Despite his constant flirting, I knew he didn't. "See something you like?" he teased.

I nodded, a teasing smile curving my lips. "Yeah, I've always wanted a six-pack," I told him and smacked my own midsection which wasn't flat at all but rather slightly rounded.

The terrible tease patted his hard flat stomach and said, "Here's one. You want it, you got it."

I shook my head and laughed. "One day I'm going to take you up on that offer and watch how quickly you run in the opposite direction." I slid off the bed and stood over him, touching the wound for any signs of tension or swelling. Touching him like this was torture because I knew it was as close as I'd ever come to touching him the way I wanted to.

"You might be surprised at my reaction, Cherie. Why don't you try it one day and find out?"

I froze for just a fraction of a second, but it was too long. I heard his chuckle, and the damn man knew he'd gotten to me. I continued checking his wound and maybe I took an extra second to enjoy the feel of his hot, hard body beneath my fingers. "You need to finish those antibiotics. Have you been taking them regularly?"

"Yes."

"Then you should be just about out. Take one a day until they're all gone, and you should be fine. Call me if you feel pain or swelling at the wound site." He let me rinse the wound with saline and pat it dry without so much as a groan. "It looks good, but we still need to keep an eye on it."

With a sleepy smile, he grabbed my wrist. "Thank you, Cherie."

"My pleasure. Can't have my hero getting an infection, can I?" For as long as I can remember he'd been my hero, and it didn't look like it would change anytime soon.

"Has anyone been bothering you?"

"No," I told him with an indulgent smile. "I made some food and left it in the oven, make sure you eat before taking those pain pills."

"Want to join me?"

"I'd love to, but I've been awake since yesterday morning, and I need my sleep." Which was exactly what I did when I got home.

And I absolutely did not dream about a certain blue-eyed, tattooed devil with a hero complex.

***

Roddick

Pulling up to the nondescript task force building, I hopped off my bike and started for the door. Mick and I made the first purchase, two bricks of heroin, from Lazarus less than an hour ago, and I was here to keep up my end of the bargain. "Agent Brockton," I told the middle-aged woman in bright red lipstick who sat behind the desk in the lobby.

He came down a few minutes later flashing his superhero fucking smile that made me itch to punch him. He was a nice guy even if he was a pretty boy. "Come on back. How'd it go?"

RODDICK

"The deal was done and there was no guy in a fancy suit introducing himself as Lazarus' boss, if that's what you want to know."

Brockton laughed and led me into a room where Agent Pollyanna waited. "Good. You have the goods?"

I slid the drugs across the table and grabbed a chair, ripping the wire off and dropping it on the table. "Everything you need is all there."

"Not quite. We need you to see if you can get us ears or eyes inside one of his stash houses." Johnson wore a shit-eating grin I'd happily smack off her if I was in the habit of putting my hands on women.

"No fucking way! That little dude is completely fucked in the head, and I ain't letting him kill or fuck me so you can make your case."

"But he's so sweet on you," she joked.

I ignored her teasing. "Well, it ain't fucking happening, so find another way." Everyone knew Lazarus was a paranoid motherfucker, moving safe houses in the middle of the night, booby-trapping them and sometimes he flat out burned it to the ground before letting someone get close enough to ID it.

Molly stood, gassing herself up to argue with me, I was sure. She'd learn real soon that I couldn't be bullied. "You're not running things here, biker boy."

"And neither are you, Pollyanna."

Brockton stepped in to break us up. "We'll put trackers in the cash and hope it will lead us to at least a few different locations. Maybe someone else in the organization."

"The money guy?" Brockton nodded. "Fine. I'll talk to Lazarus and set something up, but I need a week or he'll get suspicious." The club couldn't go from buying no drugs to selling off kilos in just a few days.

"Fine. We'll touch base in eight days."

I nodded and made my way out of the building. My phone rang, and I smiled. "Baz man, where the fuck are you?"

RODDICK

He laughed that psychotic laugh of his. "Missed me?"

"Like I missed a bullet in my side, brother."

He sobered. "This crew has some custom work they want to have done, and they're willing to pay, Rod. A lot."

I knew what he was asking and because the man could fix, upgrade, hack and manipulate any piece of hardware or software on the planet, I agreed. "Fine. Stay and finish it up."

"How's Cherie? She said you helped her with some asshole at work?"

"She's fine. Working too damn much, but I saw her two days ago when she cleaned my wound and changed my bandage." Neither of us said a thing for a long moment. "I'll look after her."

"I have no doubt or I wouldn't have asked. I gotta go, I just wanted to check in and make sure everything is cool?"

"Yep. Cherie's in good hands."

"I'm sure she is," he snickered and ended the call.

I jumped on my bike and headed for the clubhouse. I'd barely killed the engine when Torch came up to me wearing a scowl with several frowning prospects behind him. "What now?"

"Some fucked up shit is happening at the ER. I don't know what, but Minx called from another floor and said the ER is on lockdown. She saw Cherie there earlier."

Shit. Fuck. "Torch, let's go, you follow me. Prospects, watch the rear exits and don't let anyone leave. Keep an eye out for Cherie." We all got back on our bikes and burned rubber to get there. I left my bike right in front of the ER, plowing through the automatic glass doors to find most of the staff gathered around the main desk. "What's going on?"

A redhead I recognized came forward nervously. "Two Hispanic guys stormed into the ER with guns and locked themselves in one of the patient rooms with Cherie inside."

RODDICK

"A female patient?" She nodded and took a step back. "Thanks. Torch, let's go." I signaled to the prospects to stay alert and watch our sixes.

"Excuse me, but you can't…" A dark haired doctor stepped forward but went silent at the deadly look I sent his way. "The door is locked from the inside, but these keys will unlock it automatically." He handed me a white card and stepped back.

"Thank you. I promise not to make a mess of your hospital. Call Sheriff Darlington." Torch and I made our way to the locked door, pressing our ears to the door to see if we could get an idea what the fuck was going on in there. "You hear anything?" I whispered.

Torch put a finger to his lips and pointed back toward the door. Round blue eyes looked through me as he listened intently, his focus deadly. Then Cherie spoke.

"She has a bad infection and can't be moved. She was unconscious when she came in from the shock of her injuries." Her smooth whiskey voice was calm and slow, but I heard the underlying annoyance she did nothing to hide as she lied to them.

"*Puta!*" A heavily accented voice yelled, deeper than the guy who came after her in the parking lot. "Just tell us what she said, and you can go. One of your friends already told us she was talking when she came in."

I held my breath waiting for her to respond. "That's true, but she was screaming in pain but I don't speak Spanish."

"Lying bitch!" I heard the smack and Cherie's loud cry before I heard a male voice roar in pain. "I'm gonna kill you, bitch!"

That was all I needed to hear. Torch slid the white card against the reader on the wall, and we both hoped like hell the commotion hid the sound of the automatic lock. We rushed in with guns drawn on both men, each of us going for one of the bastards holding Cherie. One of them was splayed on the floor holding his neck where a syringe stuck out. He squirmed around trying to get to his feet, but Torch kicked him in the side the pressed his boot down on his neck and pinned him in place. "Stay down, motherfucker. You fucked with the wrong nurse. You okay, sweetheart?"

Cherie gave a small smile to Torch who happily treated her like she was also his kid sister. They made an odd pair, Torch with his bald head and big blue eyes, tattoos everywhere and six feet six frame, and Cherie so tiny and blonde. "I'm good. Thanks, guys." She flashed me a quick smile before turning back to the woman in the bed, but not before I saw the blush staining her cheeks. "I used my sedative on that asshole, and she needs it."

Torch and the prospects took the men before the police arrived, and I stayed behind with Cherie. "What do you need?"

She turned to me, taking several deep breaths that drew my attention to the swell of her tits under those boxy scrubs. "Sedatives. I need sedatives." She tried to step around me but, bastard that I was, I pushed forward slightly so she had no choice but to brush up against me as she shouted a few medical terms out the door. "Thanks for your help, Rod, but you can't be back here."

I was momentarily struck mute by the husky sound of my shortened name on her lips, and I imagined that's how she'd sound as I slid my hard dick inside her wet pussy.

"Roddick."

I blinked a few times. "Right. I'll be waiting for you in the lobby. Don't leave without me."

Several emotions flashed in her eyes; chief among them annoyance but also gratitude, affection and maybe even lust. Or maybe that was just wishful thinking. Instead of arguing, she smiled and gave a crisp nod. "Okay. And seriously Rod, thank you."

"Anytime, Cherie." She threw me a look I couldn't decipher before turning back to the patient as another nurse rushed in carrying a shiny silver tray. I made my way to the ER waiting room and took a seat facing the door, watching for anything that didn't sit right with me.

RODDICK

Right now, it felt like that was every goddamn thing.

KB Winters

Chapter Three

Cherie

It might sound old-fashioned to some people, but being in the kitchen relaxed me. Soothed me. And I needed it after everything that had happened at the hospital a few days ago. I was able to get Monica settled and checked in on a few other patients before leaving. The nursing administrator, Darla, insisted I take a few days off and I happily obliged, cleaning and tinkering around the house. Looking for jobs. In fact, I kept to myself. Mostly. I would've done a damn good job at it except Roddick stopped by every day with some excuse or another.

Whether I wanted him to or not.

Today I just wouldn't open the door for him. I'd ignore the ringing bell, the sound of the knocker. The man disrupted my ability to think or be smart. Act smart. Which was why I found myself in the kitchen whipping up my famous spicy fajitas with the habanero salsa Torch had taught me to make when I was far too little to enjoy the heat. He'd taught me a lot including how to cook, how to shoot a gun, and how to curse like a sailor. Which had been a million years ago before he'd taken a twelve-year-old me bra shopping. I'd just added some mint to the salsa when the doorbell rang, and I groaned.

Wiping my hands on a towel, I pushed through the kitchen door into the living room and to the front door. I knew who it would be, but I still peeked between the curtains before reluctantly opening the door. "Roddick, what a surprise," I told him, not sounding at all surprised.

"Really…" He smiled as he pushed past me to get inside. "I've been checking on you every day."

"I'm aware, but you do realize that I am a grown woman, perfectly capable of looking after myself, right? Tell Baz you have better things to do." His gaze raked over me so thoroughly I was sure he'd grown another hand that caressed me.

One side of his mouth kicked up in that lazy grin, drawing attention to the days of stubble he hadn't bothered with. "Oh, I'm aware that you're all woman, Cherie. Well aware. And Baz didn't send me."

"So. why the hell are ya here?"

"What smells so good?"

I rolled my eyes at his change of topic. "That would be the meal you interrupted." He just stood there smiling at me, casting his bright light like always. "I suppose you're angling for an invitation?"

With a deep, rumbling laugh, he pulled me into his chest and dropped a kiss on top of my head, pulling me through the living room and into the kitchen. "So kind of you to offer, Cherie, I would *love* to stay for dinner."

"Grab the soda from the fridge, then."

"No beer?" He frowned as he asked the question and looked at me like I was an alien.

"Haven't been to the store."

"Why didn't you call me? I would've gone for you."

"If it were that important, I would've gone myself."

He gave me an odd look and then a loud laugh erupted from him that included pounding his large fists on the table so hard the silverware shook. "I'm glad to see you're still as fiery as ever. I was worried at first that this might have shaken you."

"It did, but no more than anything else in my life." Torch was part of CAOS when he took over caring for me while Baz was away, and when Baz returned he joined CAOS too. I've been surrounded by the club most of my life, and adding the ER on top of that just meant nonstop crazy. "I just felt like being at home, Rod, nothing else."

"Okay, but if you'd called, we could be gettin' drunk right now."

That did sound really good. "Aren't you worried I might use your drunken state as an opportunity to take advantage of you?"

"Hopeful," he said, serious blue eyes looking at me like they wanted to undress me.

RODDICK

"Be serious, Rod." To stop my stupid heart from hoping, I took a big, unladylike bite of my fajita. He'd been flirting with me more and more lately, but ever since Baz had woken me up in the middle of the night with news that Roddick had been shot, he'd kicked it up a notch. Or maybe it was just that his wound meant we spent more time together. I'd love to believe he meant it, that he wanted me. But I knew better. So I chewed. And chewed again.

Roddick finished off three fajitas before pushing his plate away and patting a midsection I now knew was rock hard. "That was delicious, Cherie. Thanks."

"No problem. I made it just for you." I tried to stop from laughing, but the look on his face was priceless.

"In that case, I really loved it, but fuck, that salsa is spicy!" He pulled another can of soda from the fridge and drank half of it in one gulp. His big body took up so much room in my tiny kitchen that I couldn't pull my eyes from him, especially the way he leaned against the counter with his legs crossed at the ankle. "What's this?"

I froze at his words and the confusion in his tone because I knew exactly what he'd found. The classified ads I'd printed out so I could highlight the requirements. "Those are job ads."

He glared at me. "But none of them are even in California."

"Yes, that's kind of the point. As soon as I fulfill my specialty hours at the hospital, I'm leaving Brently." I knew instantly he didn't like that idea, and I wanted to know why. But I was a chicken shit, so I didn't ask.

"Why?"

There were plenty of reasons, but the main one was staring at me with confusion and hurt in his eyes. I could give him any of the other reasons I'd come up with to tell people when they found out, but I didn't want to lie to Roddick. "Why not?"

He crossed his arms over his chest, glaring at me like he was trying to figure me out, which was weird because there was no mystery to me. "Why don't you like me, Cherie? Have I done something?"

"What?" I couldn't possibly have heard him right. "I like you just fine, Roddick. In fact, I've had a pretty big crush on you for most of my life." I'd been a little obsessed from the moment I saw him, so big and tall and tough. "I've been taking care of you, making sure you don't die, and endured all of your teasing flirtations, so what makes you think I don't like you?"

He shrugged and leaned on the table with flat palms so his face was so close I could see the flecks of gold and silver mixed into the blue of his eyes. "You always seem frustrated around me, and I want to know why."

I couldn't help but laugh because it was more sexual frustration, but he didn't need to know that. "You're always teasing me."

"It's called flirting."

Now I really wished I had a beer or two around. "No, it's called flirting when you want something to come of it, otherwise, it's just teasing."

"And you think I don't?"

I nodded. I couldn't even open my mouth to admit that I knew he didn't want me, that he just teased me like I was still that little girl with a crush. Which I guessed I was. "I know it, Rod." Pushing my chair back with a little too much force, I stood and began to clean up.

"You don't know shit, girl." Before I could tell him to watch how he talked to me, big hands grabbed me and spun me around, trapping me between his big, hard body and the sink.

Then his lips were on mine, so soft and so firm. Commanding. Spicy, as his tongue dragged against my bottom lip and pulled it between his teeth, forcing a gasp from me. Then, sweet heaven on a platter, his tongue swept into my mouth hungrily, tangling with my own and exploring the depths of my mouth. God, his mouth felt like...*everything*. His lips teased me while his tongue drove me straight out of my mind, a spicy, sweet frenzy a girl could get used to.

My hands slid up his abs and over his pecs before curling around his neck to bring him closer. My hands played in his hair, and in an act of bold sensuality I pulled his tongue into my mouth and sucked it, the way I'd dreamed of sucking him for so long. The feel of his big hands gripping my ass sent my mind swirling with thoughts of getting naked with him. But he pulled back entirely too soon. "I wouldn't joke about wanting you, Cherie. I've spent too many years denying myself."

I stood there like a silent fool while he brushed his thumb across my bottom lip before turning on his heels and leaving me a pile of lust and want.

And totally unsatisfied.

Story of my life.

Roddick

"Not that I'm not completely giddy with excitement that I've lured you over to the dark side, Roddick, but why the change of heart?" Lazarus had been teasing and flirtatious to the point of discomfort, but I knew his game so I played it cool while he played with the fancy scarf tied around his neck.

"The boys are getting older and have families, and just a year of this shit could set us all up nicely." It would've been the truth if the whole club knew about this, but since it wasn't a permanent thing, just a select few were in on it.

He looked skeptical in his shiny gray suit with a pink silk top opened to the sternum to show off a bony, hairy chest. "I'll give you a few kilos to start, see how fast you can move them. You do well and Lazarus will hook you up nicely, okay? Okay." He twirled and clapped twice, sharply to move his men into action.

RODDICK

"Sounds good. Thank you, Lazarus." Despite our differences, we'd managed a decent relationship all these years because the man was like a spinster aunt—a smile and a few good manners went a long way.

One of his men dressed in black from head to toe handed two kilos to Mick, and we headed out of the same building in the center of the same crowded market we'd met at in the past. The place was empty except a few tables and chairs along the scuffed wood. "I hope you know what you're doing, man. This is a dangerous game after all of the shit we've been through." Mick let out a long, low whistle, and I nodded because he was right. This shit would either clear the club of the police for a long time and set us up for a good long while, or we'd all end up dead.

"I know and that's why things have to be this way, Mick. If we don't do this now we'll be fighting the cartels, specifically the Mexican Devils, until the day we die. I can't live knowing CAOS died on my watch." I didn't want it to be this way, none of it, but I loved my club enough to ensure they still had a future. "It'll work out, Mick, you'll see."

His response was a dissatisfied grunt as he started his bike. I did the same, and we met up with Cash and Torch a few blocks over for the quick trip back over the border into Brently. The boys were done, but I still needed to call Brockton, which I did as soon as I made it back to my place, which smelled suspiciously like chili. And cornbread.

I pulled out my piece because while I doubted a killer would break in and cook me a meal, someone had still been inside my fucking house without my permission. "Anybody in here?" I'd hate to shoot one of the prospects, but they'd better speak up. "Shit," I sighed when I found the kitchen empty and clean with a note anchored down by a jar of jalapeno peppers.

"Maybe I'll invite myself over for dinner next time," the note read. It wasn't signed, but it didn't take a genius to figure out who had written it.

RODDICK

With a goofy smile on my face, I called Brockton. "We made another buy, not even an hour ago."

"Great. We've already got some intel from your last one. I'll swing by tomorrow to get them."

"Yeah and make sure you're discreet." The last thing I needed was for my neighbors to think I was working with the cops. Or dating a dude.

"Yeah, I always am," he joked, and we both laughed. The man couldn't *not* look like a cop if that were his job.

"I guess that's why they don't let you do undercover work."

"Right. Tomorrow then, Roddick."

When the call ended, I was too keyed up to sleep. Too restless to sit on the sofa with my feet propped up on the nicked coffee table to watch TV and unwind.

Somehow, I found myself in the truck I kept for errands, and ten minutes later I was parked outside the little ranch house with yellow and blue shutters

Cherie had moved into a few years ago. She could have stayed with Baz but the man was a pussy hound, and she'd gotten sick of dealing with spurned lovers, outraged exes, and all night fuck sessions. I didn't want to just show up unannounced, but I needed to see her after that kiss we shared. I sent her a text with just one word. "Outside."

Fuck, I hadn't stopped thinking about that kiss for the past couple days. Her sweet, succulent lips so ready to receive pleasure, so ready to taste me. Touch me. My dick grew hard just thinking about the way her round ass felt in my hands. The weight of it, the softness.

"Do you want to be inside?"

I smiled at her message. "So bad." Then I was at the door, and she pulled it open looking all sexy and fuckable in tiny workout shorts and a fitted tank that showed off every one of her mouthwatering curves.

"Yes?"

"Invite me in, Cherie," I growled, my gaze glued to hers as we stood staring at each other and wondering if tonight would be the night we finally acted on the chemistry we both tried to deny for years. Too many fucking years.

"Why?"

"Invite me in and see," I told her and held up the pot of chili she made for me. "This might be a good place to start."

Cherie stepped back and brushed a blonde curl from her face. "Or maybe to finish," she said, punctuating the final words by turning the lock. "Why are you here, Roddick?"

Why was I here? We both knew why. Setting the pot down, I turned to her and grinned. "I came for you, Cherie, for this," I told her and fixed my mouth over hers, kissing her deep and slow until I felt the hitch in her breath when my hand found a beaded nipple to play with while my mouth roamed the playground of hers. She tasted sweet and salty, like sex personified. I used my height advantage to press her against the wall, to press my growing cock into her. "Feel what you do to me, Cherie. How hard I am for you."

A sexy, tortured moan escaped her, and I swear my cock grew harder. "Oh, I feel," she said, sounding all breathy like I'd already fucked her senseless.

Not yet.

"My turn to feel." I grabbed the hem of her tank and pulled it over her head, casting my gaze on her big tits squished together in a sports bra. I tugged on the zipper in front and took that off too, and damn near choked on the breath I took. They were big, a D cup and shaped like a tear drop so her nipples aimed right at my mouth. "Fuck, Cherie, your tits are gorgeous." Grabbing them in my hands, squeezing the soft, milky flesh so I could taste the raspberry buds now hard and straining toward me.

"Oh god," she moaned right in my ear, sending another shot of lust straight to my cock. "Yes, please!" Her delicate hands speared through my hair to hold me close. Like I was going any fucking where with those gorgeous tits on display, growing harder and heavier as I worked them over.

But goddammit, it wasn't enough. I lifted her in my arms, loving the way she squealed my name in surprise. "I need to lay you out, Cherie. Taste and love you properly." Before she could say a word though, we were in her room, and I tossed her on the bed. "I love the way your tits jiggle."

She smiled up at me, chest heaving with the effort it took her to breathe through her arousal. "Do you?" she asked innocently and gave a little shimmy that made them jiggle more.

"Don't," I yelled at her when she went to remove her shorts. "Let me." I grabbed her ankle and pulled her to the edge of her queen-size bed. "Your skin is so fucking soft, like rose petals." My hands grazed up and down her soft, feminine body. It was these curves that had done me in the year she turned seventeen, wearing a short plaid skirt with calf-high Doc Martens looking like my own twisted version of the naughty schoolgirl. Now I had her right here, trembling under my hands, and I planned to make the most of it.

"Rod," she moaned when my knuckles brushed against the swollen lips of her pussy. "Please."

"Please what, Cherie?"

"Stop teasing me."

I laughed and dropped to my knees. "Oh, I haven't even started to tease you, sweetheart." Grabbing the waistband of her shorts, I pulled them off along with the lacy panties she wore underneath and inhaled. "So sweet." Spreading her legs, I groaned at the sight she made, all pink and bare and wet. Throbbing. "So fucking wet. Is that all for me?" I knew it was, and I couldn't wait a second longer to bury my face in that sweet, fat pussy and lick her until she screamed my name.

"Oh shit!"

Her fingers twirled around my hair, not pulling or pushing me either way, just holding on to me like I was the only thing keeping her tethered to earth. She was soaked and dripping down my throat and chin, but I didn't give a shit. I thrust my tongue deep inside her cunt, fucking her while she squirmed under my mouth.

"Roddick, I—" She didn't finish the sentence because she couldn't. Because I sucked her clit and speared her pussy with my fingers until she flew apart wildly, clenching my fingers and flooding the space between us with her juices. "Oh. My. God. That was amazing," she shrilled as her body continued to shiver and convulse.

"And that was just the warm up." I kissed my way up her body, giving her tits extra love before I descended on her mouth. "Want to know how good you taste?"

She was hesitant at first but then I spotted it, that gleam in her eyes that said she was ready to accept the challenge. She grabbed my face with both hands and she didn't just kiss me, she devoured my mouth, licking and sucking my tongue until it was clear of all traces of her. "Different but I like the taste of us together."

I groaned, "Sweetheart, you're killin' me." She didn't even know how she had me going, my dick was trying to break out of my pants.

"Then I'd say it's time for you to dress for the party." Her gaze landed on my fully clothed body, and she flashed me a sexy grin.

I jumped off the bed and made quick work of my clothes, only pausing when she sucked in a breath at the sight of my cock jutting out before I climbed back on the bed beside her. "Like what you see, Cherie?"

"You know I do, Roddick." She reached for my cock, soft hands stroking gently until my balls pulled up tight. "I like it a lot."

"Take it."

"Give it to me," she groaned when I moved between her legs, rubbing the tip of it against her drenched opening. "Now."

My cock sank into her slowly. Inch by torturous inch until I met with... impossible. "There something you want to tell me, sweetheart?"

"Besides I'm a virgin?"

"No," I groaned, struggling to remain still, but she was so fucking wet and tight and hot. "That's what I meant. Why didn't you—"

"Say something? You were making me feel too good, and if you stop now I might kill you myself."

"Yeah," I laughed and kissed her while my body sank deep inside her tight sheath, swallowing her cry of pain. "You okay?"

"I will be," she exhaled a long breath. "If you move. Please."

That was all the permission I needed to plunge balls deep inside her body, clenching and squeezing me. "Cherie," I growled because being inside of her made me feel like an animal. Pulling out I plunged in again slower and deeper, again and again as her cries grew louder. More tortured. Fuck she felt too good, and I knew I wouldn't hold out much longer, so I lifted her thighs and tossed them over my forearms, plunging deeper and faster while my thumb rubbed circles into her clit. "Come for me, Cherie."

She nodded, mouth open and swollen, eyes glazed over with lust. One more thrust and she flew apart, crying my name until her voice went hoarse. "Wow. Holy shit." Her body shook with laughter that was quickly interrupted by my continued strokes into her body. "Oh, oh wow. I think I'm—" Her words were cut off once again, lost forever to the way I made her feel. Another rough thrust and a pinch to her clit, and she was coming again, all over my cock.

"I can feel you pulsing around me. Milking my cock dry because you want it all, don't you?"

"Yes."

I thrust again, harder. "Don't you?"

"Yes. I want it, Roddick. I want it all."

And fuck if that didn't send me up and over the edge, one final thrust into her as I emptied myself into her pulsing cunt. "Fuck, Cherie." Hell, I couldn't think coherently.

RODDICK

"Oh, God, Roddick. That was un-fucking-real. My body is still buzzing."

That made me want to stay here forever. Right inside her tight, wet cunt. I rolled over and brought her with me, taking her mouth in a kiss that had me hard and pulsing all over again. Fuck, I was already addicted to her. "What I need to know, Cherie, is how in the hell are you still a virgin?"

"I'm not anymore. You took care of it for me." She grinned in that cheeky way she had that made me want to shake her and kiss her.

"That still doesn't answer my question."

She sat up and rested her hands on my chest and her chin on top of her hands so we were eye to eye. "When would I have had the chance with a big bad biker gang harassing any guy I wanted to go out with? You guys made it impossible to date, so it's only fair you gave this gift to me."

"Fuck that, Cherie, you gave *me* a gift and don't ever fucking forget that." She nodded and laid her head on my chest. Moments later I could tell she'd fallen asleep by her deep breathing.

Then the fucking guilt hit me. As amazing as this night was, as incredible and life changing as it had felt to be buried deep inside her, I felt like six kinds of asshole. She was Baz's kid sister, and he was my brother in arms, which meant she was off limits. Only tonight I couldn't resist her. Twenty-two-years younger than me and a fuckin' virgin to boot, and I couldn't fucking resist her. I never fucking stood a chance, but fuck me, I didn't regret it. I couldn't regret it, even now.

But I needed to think. To wrap my mind around what had happened and figure out what would happen next. What *could* happen next. I held her in my arms a little longer, letting the smell of her seep into my skin, into my soul.

Then I got dressed and went home.

RODDICK

***

Cherie

The long drive back to Brently was just what I needed after the tension of the past two days. I had an interview at St. Angeles hospital, and it went very well. They were impressed with my credentials and my age, not to mention the fact that I had no husband and children to impact my dedication to the job, though they didn't say that last part. I could tell.

Unfortunately, I also knew I would not be accepting the offer when it finally came because the hospital didn't heave nearly enough nurses to handle the incoming patients. I didn't go to school to spend my whole life inside the four walls of the hospital. I wanted a life, a real life, that included friends and nights out, maybe a few dates, and eventually a relationship. With a husband and kids, too. Maybe. What I knew for certain was that I needed to get the hell out of Brently. And away from Roddick.

After years of bottling up my feelings for him, I'd finally done it. I'd changed the nature of our relationship. Only instead of going from his buddy's little sister to his girlfriend, I'd made the much smaller, much more insignificant leap to one-night stand. Not even the kind of one-night stand where you have sex again before breakfast is finished cooking, but the kind where you sneak out in the middle of the fucking night.

But I wouldn't be upset about it. Or hurt. I'd treat it as a lesson learned because that would make leaving California easier. Even though the job interview was a bust, it had taken the edge off, and now I wouldn't be nervous for future interviews.

The only thing that made my heart ache was the thought of leaving Baz. Other than his stint in the military, we hadn't spent any significant time apart. Hell, even his stint back east was more time than we'd spent apart in our whole lives, and it would be hard to live without him. But I had to do it. Maybe I would end up in Chicago or St. Louis or maybe some small town in Michigan. Anywhere, really. The world was my oyster as they say.

RODDICK

By the time I arrived home I felt like I needed a stiff drink and a horror movie marathon, but as soon as I got settled on the sofa my phone rang. I looked at the screen and groaned because I knew what was coming next. "Hey, Darla."

"Cherie, how are you doing?"

I rolled my eyes. Darla meant well, but what she really wanted to know was if I was ready to work. "I'm fine, Darla. All good."

"Oh, that's wonderful. Is there any way you could pick up an extra shift today?"

"Yes."

"Are you sure?"

"Yep." This would be another ten to twelve hours closer to meeting my obligation to the hospital. Ten hours closer to leaving Brently. "I'll see you soon, Darla."

She let out a long sigh of relief. "Oh, thank you, Cherie. We can always count on you to pitch in."

Yeah, because nearly every other nurse had a family or had one in the works. I was one of a handful of single and unencumbered nurses everyone looked to fill in, as though having a family was the only reason I might not want to work a shift. "Bye, Darla," I told her and hung up. I took a minute to catch my breath before pushing off the sofa and padding to the bedroom where I changed into a pair of clean scrubs. I dumped yogurt, granola, and berries into a bowl and packed it in my bag for lunch, then grabbed my sweater before heading out. A quick glance at the clock told me I didn't have time to stop at Black Betty's for coffee so I went back for a soda even though I was trying hard to get over my love of the sugary carbonated beverage. It was the last one in the fridge so I promised to keep it that way as I pulled open the door and found Roddick standing on my doorstep with his fist ready to knock.

God, had it only been two days since I'd seen him? I drank in the sight of him, every delicious inch of his broad shoulders and long muscular legs. My mind instantly recalled the way the tattoo on his neck tasted on my tongue, the way his muscles bunched and flexed under my hands. The sight he made naked, the Roman guard tattoo making him look every inch the fierce warrior he was. And as quickly as those images came so did the feelings he evoked—the heat, the tension, the need to have him inside me again. The humiliation of waking up alone. "What are you doing here?" I asked, hip checking him aside so I could step out and lock the door.

"What's the hurry?" He smiled under that day old scruff that made him look even sexier, damn him.

"Work," I answered, refusing to look up at him again if for no other reason than my own sanity. I jogged down the five steps on my stoop in my hurry to put some distance between us.

"You don't have time to talk?"

"I don't." Talking wouldn't help anything anyway.

"Cherie, we need to talk."

I shoved my bag across to the passenger seat and stood, looking at him over the hood of my car.

"There's nothing to talk about, Roddick. It happened. You left. It's done. Goodbye." I jumped into my car, started the engine, and peeled out of the driveway much faster than I should have, but I needed to get away from him before he convinced me to hear whatever bullshit reason he'd taken two days to formulate about why he left in the middle of the night.

I could feel his gaze on me, but I chanted to myself—*I will not look back, I will not look back*. Because I didn't care that he was left standing there confused and maybe a little hurt. I didn't kid myself that he was hurt at all, probably just pissed that I didn't let him control the situation.

I looked back anyway.

And I hated myself for it.

The man would always have a piece of me, which meant the sooner I got away the better it would be for my heart. My peace of mind.

Chapter Four

Roddick

"What the fuck, man?" Within seconds of locking my front door, I had my piece in my hand aimed at the man twiddling his fucking thumbs in my favorite burgundy leather recliner. The chair sat in the corner giving me the perfect view out the window, at the television, and of both entrances to my house. I accused Lazarus of being paranoid, but I had a healthy amount of it myself. It came with being a soldier and an outlaw.

Brockton smiled that smug smile of a Fed, not seeming all that worried about the gun aimed at his head. "I needed a meeting, and you weren't answering your phone."

"Whatever the fuck you believe, Brockton, I don't sit around waiting for you to blow up my phone." The man had a death wish because if he pulled this shit again, I'd pull the fucking trigger.

"We have a location on the money for the first drop, and we need another. At least three." He looked at me expectantly, like I was supposed to jump in the air and click my fucking heels together.

"Why?"

"So we can watch the locations and track the cash."

These Feds thought everything was so goddamn easy because they never learned to plan for the worst. "And you don't think Lazarus will get suspicious about where all of our new buyers are coming from since we've been against drugs from the beginning?"

Brockton's lips curled again, full of smug confidence. "Absolutely not. He only cares about the money, end of story. Keep it coming and he'll keep you flush with drugs." He pulled two large bricks of cash from the bag on the floor and smacked them on the table, taking the drugs I'd retrieved from a hiding place in my bedroom.

"If you really think that then this operation is in more trouble than I thought." I grabbed two beers from the fridge, surprise flashed in my eyes when Captain America took one. I popped the cap on my bottle and took a seat. "You might be right about Lazarus having a boss, but he's not just paranoid, he's careful. If this shit comes back on the club, we're gonna have problems." It wasn't a threat. It was a promise.

"I know you CAOS boys don't think too highly of the government, but we're good at what we do, Roddick."

"I think you might actually be good at your job, Brockton, but you don't know how a guy like that thinks. Imagine how ruthless, how intelligent a flamboyant guy like that has to be to stay at the top for so long." I didn't know a single gay man in any of the organizations we dealt with never mind at the top. "He cares about money, but I promise you he cares about his freedom more."

"Maybe so, but we've got this under control."

"You think you do, but I guess we'll see in the end. Have you checked your task force for vulnerabilities because the Devils have people everywhere?"

I saw that hint of concern in his eyes, but I decided not to go there. "It's under control."

"Whatever." I finished my beer and a stood, a clear sign that it was time for him to go. "I'll call you soon."

He thanked me for the beer and left through the backdoor, along the trails behind my house so no one would see him. When he was long out of sight, I grabbed another beer and contemplated going back to the clubhouse. We still had prospects to deal with, and if things went the way they were supposed to, we needed them to be ready. But after spending all day there all I wanted to do was relax with a soft warm woman Too bad the only woman I wanted in my arms was currently pissed as hell at me, and rightfully so. The way she looked at me right before she dropped down in her car left me feeling gutted, wrung out. Hurt and disappointment shone in her big brown eyes, and there was more than a hint of anger in those depths. I deserved her anger, goddammit, but I was worried about her. She hadn't responded to any of my calls or texts which pissed me off. And on top of ducking my attempts to contact her, she was never home when I stopped by. She was definitely avoiding me.

And what did I expect, taking her virginity and then leaving in the middle of the night? If someone else had done that to her, I'd be the first in line to kick his ass. It didn't matter that I freaked out like a fucking little boy and ran away. She didn't deserve me leaving in the middle of the night, and she sure as shit didn't deserve the arrogant way I'd shown up like I hadn't done anything wrong.

I fucked up, and I had done so spectacularly. But I could admit that I was wrong, and I wanted to make it up to her.

If she would ever give me the fucking chance.

in my arms.

***

Shit was different when Mick and I met up with Lazarus for another exchange. For one thing, the crazy little fucker hadn't flirted with me once and I was grateful, but everyone was tense. He walked up to me holding two brown paper wrapped bricks and pushed them into my chest, letting his tiny hands graze against me. "Does this mean your little town is now a thoroughfare for our product?"

Oh, he'd fucking love that. "Hell no. I don't want this shit infecting my town or the people in it."

He laughed, clapping his hands with delight. "I understand. Not your town but other towns are okay?"

"Other towns ain't my problem."

"You boys are doing a good little business. Do you mind if I ask where you're conducting it?"

Mick growled, "So you can try to hone in on our turf? I don't fucking think so."

RODDICK

I wanted to smile at Mick's vehemence. "That's what you might call proprietary information," I told the man to appease him.

This time Lazarus tilted his head back and let loose a loud guffaw of a laugh. "Roddick, you do amuse me." He gave another quick clap of his hands before he made a shooing motion. "Off you go, boys, to make us rich. See you soon, Roddick."

I gave a quick nod, and Mick and I made our way back to our bikes and met up with Torch and Cash. After getting shot a few months back we weren't taking any fucking chances, especially if Lazarus even had a clue what we were up to.

When we got to Brently the guys took the exit toward the clubhouse, and I continued on toward that fucking office building I was growing to hate more with every meeting. The process of debriefing was long and tedious, with Brockton and Johnson throwing questions at me like I was some fucking suspect. They logged in the drugs using specific information, and by the time it was all over, hours had gone by. I knew it was important work, but fuck if I ever thought I'd be doing any kind of work for Uncle Sam again. I knew this was good work though because while I had no problem with grown men and women who willingly smoked, snorted, and injected drugs—that was their business—I had a big fucking problem with the women and girls it was forced upon to make them easier to deal with. And the kids they forced to sell that shit made me sick to my stomach. Yeah, I had a big problem with that shit.

"You did good, Roddick. This is really going to help us out." Brockton smiled and sealed the money into evidence bags.

"Yeah, no problem."

"You're a regular Boy Scout, aren't you?" Johnson smirked, but it wiped off her face when I stood to my full height and closed in on her.

"You have a big fucking mouth, little girl." Damn, I wished she were a man so I could lay her out. "You're lucky I'm not in the mood for your shit."

"What are you gonna do?"

RODDICK

"How about I let Lazarus know the Feds are looking into him? Maybe I'll tell him some agent named Molly Johnson is asking questions." Her already pale skin paled further, and that left me intrigued. Maybe it was time to dig into the little bitch.

"All right, you two, that's enough. Johnson, get out." She sneered and flounced out as Brockton raked a hand through his hair. "Ignore her, Roddick, but man you can't threaten a federal agent."

"It wasn't a threat."

He swallowed whatever he'd been about to say and nodded. "I'll call you soon, but seriously, thank you."

I didn't want his fucking thanks. I just wanted this shit to be over. With a half grunt, I walked out of the building, hopped on my bike, and didn't stop until I was parked outside Cherie's house. Of course, her car was gone and there wasn't one light on, not even to illuminate the porch.

I did the only thing I could. Dismounted my bike and sat on her porch.

Waiting like a fucking dog.

Chapter Five

Cherie

I was so exhausted I could barely keep my eyes open on the short drive home after two ten hour shifts. There were two more hours left on my shift, but thanks to a new nurse looking to make a good impression, I was able to leave early. I didn't have the heart to tell her I was the wrong person to impress since my time in town and at the hospital was limited. I don't even know how I made it home in one piece. Friday and Saturday were the worst days to work the ER, and my shifts had spanned both days, giving me a front-row seat to the worst parts of humanity.

My shifts had it all—gunshot wounds, rape kits, auto accidents and knife wounds, beatings, overdoses and more than a dozen college kids had come in with alcohol poisoning. I normally loved the ER, but the past two days made me hopeful to find a job in the mental health field. It had taken so much energy out of me that I didn't even notice the motorcycle parked beside me until I nearly knocked it over. *Dammit.* I spent too much time over the past few days trying not to think about the man who belonged on that bike, and now he was here. Somewhere. "I'm not in the mood tonight, Roddick." I brushed past him on the porch, not even lifting my head in his direction.

"Good, because I didn't come here for that." He stood and took the keys from my hand, shoving the right one into the lock and pushing the door open. "Go on," he urged, giving me a light shove into the house.

I didn't argue because I was too tired, and he'd get bored when he realized I wasn't playing his game tonight. Without a word or a backward look, I went to my bedroom to take off my clothes and headed straight for a long hot shower to wash eighteen hours of ER from my body. It felt good to be clean, free of other people's blood, spit, and vomit. I slid a thin pink t-shirt over my head. It barely covered my ass, but this was my house, and I planned to crash after a glass of water and a banana to stop the growling in my stomach. "You're still here."

RODDICK

"I am. Have a seat," he instructed and slid a plate stacked with a roast beef sandwich and balsamic vinegar chips in front of me.

"Thank you." And just like that my heart began to soften toward him because big, strong Roddick had made me a sandwich. With my own food. I must be crazy. But it felt good to have someone taking care of me like this.

"Beer or water?"

"Water, please." I could definitely use a beer, but I'd pass out after two sips. I took the tall glass filled with ice and chugged it in a most unladylike fashion, and instead of mocking me he took the glass and refilled it, sitting across from me and slowly drinking one of the pale ales. "Thanks for this, Roddick, but I can take care of myself."

"I know you can, but you seem exhausted and I'm here. You're welcome." He flashed a grin, but it faded as his expression turned serious. "I owe you a huge fucking apology, Cherie."

I shook my head, begging the tears stinging my eyes to go the hell away. "No. Not now, Rod. I just…can't."

"You can't listen?"

I shook my head, eyes closed as I used the last of my energy to finish eating. "No. Listening will require thinking, and I'm done. I'm at capacity, Roddick, what the hell?" He scooped me out of the chair and stalked back down the hall, setting me on the bed gently like I was some precious cargo instead of the girl he'd hit it and quit it with.

"Fine. We'll talk in the morning." I'd already turned away from him and curled up under the comforter when I felt the bed dip and a hot chest sear my back.

"What are you doing?"

"I'm sleeping. Don't worry, I kept my boxers on so you don't get tempted to take advantage of me in the night."

RODDICK

I let out a groan when he pulled me in tight. "If I wanted to get rid of you, that's exactly what I should do."

He said nothing for a long time, and I thought maybe he *would* get up and leave. Instead, he kissed my neck, forcing me to use all my willpower not to respond to his lips on my skin. "If you want to talk about it now, we can."

"Nope, I'm sleeping until I run out of sleep, so keep your hands to yourself."

"I don't need my hands to make you come, Cherie."

I shivered because, damn him, he was totally fucking right. "Well then, keep your tongue and your cock to yourself," I told him just as he pressed his erection against my ass. "Sleep, Rod."

"Halfway there, babe."

I rolled my eyes, but with how tired I was and the heat emanating from his body—okay, and how good it felt to be *in* his arms—I fell asleep quickly.

I woke up later, annoyed that I hadn't remembered to pull down the blackout shades, a golden hue of light peeking through the window. And then I felt the furnace at my back and soft lips making my skin shiver, my nipples pebbled with desire. I wanted to lie there for a moment and relish the feel of his lips on my flesh, but I couldn't. I had to move before he pulled me back under his spell, and it would be even harder to leave. But when I tried to get up, he only held me tighter.

"Good morning, Cherie." He turned my face to him and brushed his lips against mine. "Ready to talk?"

"Nope."

"Good, that means you're ready to listen." He dropped another sweet kiss on my mouth, and I struggled not to whimper when he pulled back. "Cherie, I'm so damn sorry. I shouldn't have left like I did, but if I'm being honest, I freaked the fuck out. You're not just some girl. You're my friend's sister, *my* friend, and a woman I want more than I should."

RODDICK

"Yeah, well, you have a funny way of showing it." I refused to let my heart believe his words because his actions said differently.

"I took your fucking virginity, Cherie. Sweetheart, that means something."

"It means I woke up alone after experiencing some really intense emotions." I shook off the tears that threatened. "I appreciate your apology, Roddick, I really do. But it doesn't change anything between us."

He turned me on my back and fit his body between my legs, making me both happy and devastated that I didn't have underwear on. "That's where you're wrong. It changes *everything*."

"Because you say so?"

He shook his head and pressed a kiss across my collarbone. "Hell no. Because it *is* so." His mouth connected with mine, but it wasn't the fierce crash I'd been expecting. Instead, it was a slow and sensual coming together, a simmering heat that began at the spot where our lips met and spread as our tongues and hands explored.

His kiss made me desperate for more of him, made me cling to his big shoulders as his lips kissed up and down my body, making me tremble. A distant voice told me to stop this nonsense, to push him away, and kick him out. But a closer voice, the hussy inside of me, silenced that voice and told me to take what I wanted from this man. To enjoy every swipe of his tongue across my pussy, every squeeze of his hands on my breasts. "Rod!"

He groaned when I tugged on his hair, the sound vibrating my clit and pushing me closer to the edge. I felt entirely too much, and Roddick took advantage, broad shoulders pushing me wide open and fucking me with his tongue while his fingers squeezed my nipples. It should hurt, but it felt so good I crawled up the bed. "Oh no you don't, Cherie. Stay right here." He pulled me back and palmed my open thighs, flattening his tongue so I couldn't look away as he tasted me, licked me. "Tell me how much you like this, Cherie."

RODDICK

"I love it." His tongue swirled around my clit, a delicious tornado of sensations that made me wetter.

"More," he growled, stabbing my opening with his tongue.

"Roddick, I love when you lick my pussy. Seeing my juices on your face makes me horny." I felt a blush stain my body at the naughty words I'd never used. "Oh, shit!" He wrapped his lips around my clit and sucked until fireworks went off behind my eyes, and my body convulsed violently.

"Absolutely beautiful," he growled.

"Now it's my turn." I smiled. "I've been thinking about sucking your cock since I knew it was something men and women did."

He groaned and fell back on the bed beside me, but I quickly popped up, suddenly energized at the thought of making him moan and scream my name. "I don't think I'll last long with your sweet lips wrapped around my cock."

"That's okay. I won't judge." Suddenly I felt confident as I shimmied down his body, pulling down his boxers and holding the hard length in my hand. "You like a soft touch," I asked with a gentle stroke, "or a harder one?" I squeezed harder and gave a rough tug.

"Fuck yes, Cherie."

I smiled and leaned in, swiping my tongue across the drop of pre-come shining from the head of his cock. "Mmm, kind of salty and earthy." He groaned again, hips moving as I slowly took him all the way down my throat. Testing the feel of him in my mouth was a strange sensation, the skin was silky smooth but his cock was rock hard. When I did something he liked, his cock pulsed on my tongue, and I felt my pussy gush with more slick.

"Yeah, Cherie, just like that." One hand went to my head, but he didn't push me down; instead, he helped me maintain the right pace. Grunting and moaning his satisfaction, his hips bucked when he touched the back of my throat. "Fuck, Cherie."

RODDICK

I was intoxicated, drunk on the taste of him, and I couldn't stop. His sounds boosted my confidence and my arousal, and I experimented, pumping his cock with my hand while I explored his sack with my tongue.

"Cherie, no more!" He pulled me up by the arms, running my drenched pussy back and forth across his cock.

"Oh!"

"Sit on my cock. Ride me, Cherie."

I shivered at his words. How did he make it sound so dirty, and why did it turn me on so much? I didn't know, but I knelt over him and gripped him in my hand, slowly sinking down on his impressive length until I was so full I clenched around him. Another orgasm was imminent. "Oh God!"

"Fuck, that feels so good. Your cunt is so tight."

In a slow and probably clumsy up and down motion, I felt my way around this, feeling so full I almost couldn't stand it. Almost, but it felt too good to stop. Faster and faster I bounced, impaling myself with every move as my orgasm pushed to the surface. "Fuck me, Roddick. I feel so full," I panted and he gripped my hips, pounding up into me. The only sounds were the smacking of skin and our erotic grunts that only turned me on more, and soon my orgasm crashed through me like a million gallons of ocean water.

"Oh yeah," he growled and swore at the way my pussy squeezed around his cock. His hips moved at a speed I was sure wasn't possible for a normal man, but he thrust up into me hard and deep, sending another wave of pleasure through me. "Fuck! Cherie, yes!"

I opened my eyes because I needed to see this moment. His face twisted into a pained expression for a brief moment then it softened and pure bliss washed over him, making him look more beautiful than I had ever seen. "You look gorgeous when you come."

RODDICK

He flashed a smile that made my heart flutter. "Thank you, babe, but I'm pretty sure you're the one with the beautiful 'O' face."

I laughed and collapsed on top of him, kissing his chest and licking his nipples, enjoying the way he shivered. "You taste good."

"So do you, Cherie." He squeezed my ass and slipped deeper inside me. "And you're mine."

I tried not to let my hope soar too much at his words, but for the rest of the day, that word resonated in my head.

Mine.

***

Roddick

"What? No fucking way! You Feds need to have your head examined." I stood and paced inside Brockton's office. These people were fucking doing my head in.

"I think you've forgotten who's in charge here," Agent Johnson bit out smugly.

"And I think you've forgotten that I'm not afraid of you, little girl." I turned to Brockton. "Let's just use some common fucking sense here. CAOS has just gotten into the drug game what, a month ago? And now we're quadrupling our orders while no one else is decreasing theirs? If you're Lazarus, what the fuck do you think is happening?"

"It doesn't matter *what* he thinks," Johnson added, punctuating her words by smacking her hand on the desk.

I ignored her. "Well?"

Brockton stared at me long and hard, his face fixed in resignation. "That you're working with the cops."

"Exactly, which puts your whole operation, not to mention my life, in jeopardy."

He nodded. "I know, Roddick, but we really need to track one, maybe two more locations to see if we can draw out the person really in charge. But we can't fucking work with the *Federales* because they're so goddamn corrupt we don't know who to trust."

"Lazarus is paranoid and suspicious of everyone. Even me. Don't fuck this up when you're so close," I told him but cut my eyes at the redheaded pain in my ass.

"I'll be in touch," he finally said, and I left, putting in a call to Mick on my way out.

"Meet me at the lookout spot," I told him before hopping on my bike and letting the warm southern California sun heat my skin. I should have used the drive back to Brently to think about Lazarus and how the hell I would help the Feds land him, but all I could think about was a curvy little blonde with a smart mouth and the sexiest most erotic cries I'd ever heard. Cherie was a revelation to me. She didn't have to work at getting my attention, she just had it. And the feel of those plump lips wrapped around my cock, watching her learn her power as a woman. Fuck. It was a heady mixture of sexy and sweet, and dammit I wanted more of it. More of her.

I meant it when I told her she was mine. I just wished things weren't so fucked up right now so we'd have time to explore it. So that I had time to talk to Baz. I wished—hell I hoped—more than anything that she wasn't serious about leaving Brently.

By the time I pulled up to the lookout spot Mick was already there, a joint perched between his lips as he leaned back on his bike. "You look like shit, man."

I grinned. "Yeah thanks, brother. I know. These fucking Feds are driving me crazy." I told him all about their ridiculous plan. "How they ever arrest anyone is a goddamn mystery to me." He passed me the joint, and I took two long pulls. "How's Talon and the baby?"

His serious expression softened and he smiled bigger than I'd ever seen, except for his wedding day. "Great. Every day I can't believe that tiny little creature is my little girl. Megan is everything."

I didn't know how to respond to that kind of emotion, so I just nodded. "Glad to hear it. They aren't the only reason I need you to stay safe Mick, got it?"

His gaze was serious again and I knew he wasn't a fan of my plan, but he was my brother in arms, my friend, so he would do what I asked.

"I've been thinking about what Brockton said about Lazarus not being the top of the pyramid, and I think they're right, but something is missing. At that last meeting, he was acting strange. More subdued, less flamboyant and flirtatious." Not that I had a problem with that, but when a man changes his demeanor there's usually a good reason. "He's on some shit, but I can't tell if it's *just* him or if there's a boss he reports to. Hell, maybe the task force has it all fucked up."

Mick nodded and stomped out the last of the joint into the soft dirt. "We need to figure this shit out before you end up dead. I'll have the guys talk to some people to see if anyone knows anything. Quietly."

We stood up there looking out over the town we had, more or less, owned and protected for decades.

I would do every damn thing in my power to do keep this one of those perfect small towns that people thought of when they thought of America. Mick's voice interrupted my thoughts.

"Do you have any guesses about his boss, if there is a boss?"

I nodded because I'd thought of nothing else since Brockton approached me. "It has to be someone with some serious juice. Who else would a guy like Lazarus fear or be willing to answer to?"

"Like a businessman?"

"Maybe, but I'm thinking someone in government with the power to make or change laws, direct law enforcement. That kind of shit."

Mick whistled. "Shit, so we might be up against the Mexican government?"

"Aren't we anyway? They're so fucking complicit in all this as it is."

"Yeah, man, but this is different. Is it worth it?"

RODDICK

"That's the million dollar fucking question, isn't it?" I told him, glancing at my phone and swearing when it buzzed. "Lazarus wants me to meet up with him Sunday morning. Alone."

"Fuck that shit, Rod. I'm coming with you, and I'm bringing Torch and Cash. We got your back."

I nodded and hopped on my bike. The men of CAOS were my brothers, my family, and I knew they'd have my back. No matter what. "Then I guess we better go talk strategy."

KB Winters

Chapter Six

Cherie

Another night in the ER and another reminder of the plague of violence upon humanity. My shift had been filled with the worst shit that we humans do to one another, and I only had ninety minutes to go. I left one room with a nine-year-old victim who had to learn much too early just how awful men could be and was called into another by the newest ER resident, Dr. Hammond. "Cherie, I need a Spanish speaking nurse, stat."

I rolled my eyes at the handsome raven-haired doctor. He was competent and good looking, but his bedside manner was for shit, and who took a medical job this close to the border with no Spanish language skills? "What have we got?" I asked instead of the other question.

"Multiple traumas, female, mid to late twenties," he rattled off without looking at the patient.

I wondered how he even knew she was female because it wasn't readily apparent based on her lopped off hair or the dirt and blood streaking her skin. "Hola, *señorita. Español o ingles?*" *Hello, miss. Spanish or English?*

The woman cast a wary glance at Dr. Hammond before her onyx gaze returned to mine. "I speak some *Ingles*," she said in a shaky voice.

I nodded and gave her the same soft professional smile I used on all my patients because it put them at ease. "What's your name?"

"Bonnie."

I nodded and kept asking questions as I took her vitals. "Are you from around here, Bonnie?"

"El Salvador is my home."

My stomach dropped at her words because there were only two reasons a woman would end up like this so far from home. Drugs or human trafficking. "Can you tell me what happened?" I asked as I continued to examine her while the doctor made notes. Bonnie was very badly beaten, one eye swollen shut and two deep gashes in her lips; blood poured from several spots on her torso and legs. Her feet were bare and, she was covered in a layer of dirt that had combined with the blood. "I need to clean you up a bit to make sure none of your wounds get infected, Bonnie, all right?"

She nodded, but the moment I began to rinse away the blood and dirt mixture, she started to scream, loud and torturous. "Oh no! Please, oh please, no more!"

"Bonnie, it's okay you're in the hospital. Everything is fine."

"I'll go get security," Hammond said as he made his way to the door.

I glared at him. "She's not causing trouble, she's in shock. If you can't handle it, go."

He happily did, and I closed the door behind him before turning back to Bonnie. "What's the matter, Bonnie, who did this to you?"

"*El Jefe* is a bad man. He is evil man who comes around in his fancy suits to punish us. We make his friends unhappy, he punish us. We get hurt, he hurt us more." Tears streaked down her cheeks, leaving a clean trail on her dirty face. "He takes time from his busy life in government to torture us."

In government? "You'll be okay here, Bonnie. Don't tell anyone what you told me," I whispered as Hammond returned.

She nodded, dark eyes growing smaller as the sedative began to kick in. I finished cleaning and disinfecting her wounds as she drifted to sleep, making sure to leave a note that she was a victim of domestic violence so I could be sure no male visitors would be allowed in her room.

By the time my shift ended, I was exhausted and in need of a decent meal and a long, hot shower. All those things were on my list, but I couldn't stop thinking about Bonnie. I knew just one person to talk to, but didn't know if I wanted to. I had no control where Roddick was concerned, but I knew if I called

Baz he'd worry and break his neck to get back here. I sucked it up and sent Roddick a message to stop by before I ticked a hot shower off my list.

"You called," he said twenty minutes later as he unpacked what I hoped was a burger from a Black Betty's bag. "I'm guessing it wasn't a personal reason?"

"Did you want it to be a personal call?" I hadn't heard from him in a couple days, so I still didn't know what was going on between us. Casual sex or something more? "Never mind. I did call for a reason, though." We worked in comfortable silence, gathering plates, barbecue sauce, and beer before we sat down to eat. Then I explained about Bonnie and what she told me.

"She said that he was *in* government?"

I nodded. "Seemed certain of it too, so I would assume he is well-known." But his reaction only brought forth more questions. "I thought maybe you could help, but I see now that this news is more than important to you."

His smile was sardonic. "Yeah, you could say that."

That was it. No sharing. No details. Nothing. I could see clearly that something about this information bothered him, his silver blue eyes practically spun he was thinking so hard. But still, he said nothing. "What's going on, Roddick? Is someone else going to end up shot? Or beaten or dead?"

He sighed and his gaze slammed into mine, filled with sorrow and fear and resignation. "I wish I knew, Cherie." He reached for my hand and pressed his lips against my knuckles so gently I nearly cried out at his tenderness. "Things are changing, and I'm trying my best to make it better for everyone. But that means things might turn to shit for a while."

"What is *a while,* Rod, a few weeks? Few months?"

"I don't know." He grabbed me and pulled me close so he could wrap his big strong arms around me. "I don't fucking know, but I wish like hell I did."

RODDICK

I let him hold me, stroke my hair, and press kisses against my head, my mouth, and my cheeks. He seemed to need the connection which surprised me, but I couldn't deny that I was happy to be the one providing it to him. But this also hammered home that I needed to keep with my plans. "This is why I'm happy that I'll be leaving town soon."

"What the hell does that mean?" He pulled back and scowled down at me.

"Exactly what I said. I'm leaving Brently for good."

"You can't leave. I won't let you!"

"Let?" I barked out a bitter laugh. "News flash, Roddick, you're not my father, my brother, or my boyfriend. You can't *let* me do anything."

"Yeah?"

I nodded as he leaned over me, bracketing me in his arms. "Yeah," I responded, feeling defiant. And a little turned on.

"You're damn right about the first two, but I think we both know you're lying to yourself about the last one."

I opened my mouth to deny it, but his mouth crashed into mine, claiming me with a heady passion I'd never felt, or dreamed of feeling. I didn't even know to dream of a kiss this consuming, slow and torturous. Soon I was lifted in the air, legs wrapped around him as he kicked the bedroom door open, dropping me on the bed and staring down at me with raw need blazing in his eyes. His gaze didn't linger, though; he undressed and then me before plunging deep into my wet, needy body. Every thrust pounded into me and pushed me closer to the edge. I gave him everything, holding nothing back and came so hard I saw stars. The only sound in the room was his deep voice growling my name as he filled me so completely I knew I'd never be whole again without him.

And my stupid heart soared at how right it felt to fall asleep in his arms. My mind just hoped like hell that he'd be there when I woke up.

RODDICK

***

Roddick

"I can't believe you're ticklish!" Cherie laughed at the way I flinched whenever her hands went to my sides. "Big tough biker man is ticklish."

"Not ticklish, woman, sensitive in that general region." She laughed again, and the sound washed over me. "What about you?" I asked and pulled her closer, tickling her and producing a husky laugh that had me hard and aching for her. Again.

"Oh I'm ticklish as hell, but you'd never exploit that, would you?" She kicked a leg across my body until she straddled me, leaking her arousal all over my own. "You feel…so good."

I groaned, holding her hips as they moved slowly, back and forth against the length of my cock. "You too, baby." She looked so beautiful with her head tossed back, her breaths coming in faster as her arousal kicked up another notch.

The doorbell rang and seconds later the door slammed, and I went on alert, reaching for my piece when a man's voice sounded. "Cherie! Where are you?"

Baz. I froze and watched as Cherie slid out of bed, casual as you please, and slid a robe over her shoulders. "I'll be right back."

I nodded and listened to the siblings talk.

"Why is Roddick's bike out front?" Suspicion laced Baz's question.

"None of your business."

"Cherie," he growled, but I knew she was one of the few people on the planet not fazed by his bark. "Don't tell me you're fucking him."

"That is none of your goddamn business, Baz, so I'm going to ask you to leave. It's early as fuck, and I've been pulling double shifts for weeks now." She did sound tired, but I knew it had more to do with the fact that we hadn't slept for more than an hour at a time because we couldn't keep our hands—and other parts—to ourselves.

RODDICK

I stood and slipped on my jeans and nothing else. "What's all the noise?" I heard the growl before his feet began to move and ducked the punch he threw my way. "What the fuck, Baz?"

"My sister? You're banging my baby sister?" He lurched forward again, but he wasn't stupid enough to throw another punch, so he just got in my face. "I fuckin' trusted you."

I held up my hands, but I wouldn't back down. "Don't act like I took advantage of her because I didn't."

"Oh yeah. You both just woke up one day and decided to fuck?"

Cherie squeezed between us and smacked her brother's face. "Will you two stop this nonsense! God!" She pushed at his chest and then mine. "*This* is why I'm leaving! Everything with you guys is a fucking fight. Use. Your. Words."

Baz scoffed, "You want words? This is fucked up! She's my sister, man!" He pushed me, and I saw the hit coming and steeled myself for it. I wouldn't hit him back because I knew I had it coming for sleeping with his sister.

"Feel better?"

"No goddammit, I don't!"

"Too bad," Cherie yelled. "Out! Get the hell out, Baz and don't come back until you can act civilized!" Tears pooled in her eyes, and I knew this visit had steeled her resolve to leave Brently.

I wrapped her in my arms and dropped a kiss on her head. "I'm so damn sorry, Cherie."

She pushed at my chest. "Don't be," she said, her head shaking and disbelief was written all over her face. "I can't believe I kicked my brother out. I picked sex over him." Watery brown eyes stared up at me, sad and disappointed. "You don't love me, and I picked you over him."

I didn't know what I felt, so I couldn't answer that accusation, but I held her face in my hands and spoke from the heart. "Sweetheart, I don't know if this is love, but I know it ain't just sex. I also know that it's not fair for Baz to make you choose. Plenty of other women your age have sex without choosing, why should you?"

"I...need to be alone." She turned away and quietly walked down the hall to her bedroom, closing the door behind her.

I would give her the space she wanted, but not like this. I followed her and dressed quickly before curling behind her on the bed and pulling her close, inhaling her sweet scent of vanilla and sex. "You mean something to me, Cherie. Something big but I won't tell you anything else until I know how this shit will turn out. It wouldn't be fair. But don't think we're done, darlin'." I turned her head and kissed her, pouring all the words I couldn't say into that kiss before pulling away and leaving, feeling torn as hell.

And pissed off about it.

KB Winters

Chapter Seven

Cherie

The past week had been complete and total hell. Baz's appearance hung a dark cloud over whatever was happening between me and Roddick. We didn't stop seeing each other because Roddick was right, it wasn't fair for Baz to expect me to choose. But it also highlighted the fact that this wasn't a forever relationship. I might have wanted it to be, but I'm not a masochist. I had to leave Brently if I ever wanted a shot at a real life away from CAOS.

But I planned to enjoy this thing with Roddick for as long as it lasted. I loved him, of that I was certain, but in the immortal words of Patty Smyth, sometimes love just ain't enough. It would hurt like hell to leave, but it was always gonna hurt. At least now I knew what it felt like to be with Roddick. To lie with a man who cared about me, because though he didnt love me, I knew he cared about me. A lot.

My shift was nearly over, so I made a quick stop to Bonnie's room. The woman had just recovered from an infection and would be discharged in the next few days. The problem was she had nowhere to go. Yet. "You're healing, Bonnie. That's very good." She cast me a half-hearted smile and squeezed my hand.

"*Gracias*, Cherie. You are very kind."

"Don't let the others hear you say that," I joked. "They'll expect me to be nice to everyone. Is there someone you'd like to call, Bonnie, you can use my phone?"

"I cannot go back to my husband and children after what they have done to me. No thank you, *Señorita*."

I squeezed her hand and gave her a quick smile before leaving her room. Ten minutes later I strode through the front doors and into the thick night air. I hardly remembered what sunlight felt like since I'd been working second and third shifts for so long. I groaned when I spotted a familiar figure leaning against my car wearing a shit eating grin. "What do you want, Baz?"

His smile vanished. "I came to apologize."

"Then let's hear it."

"I'm sorry, okay? I shouldn't have acted the way I did, but dammit, Cher…Roddick, really?"

"I don't need to justify my actions to you, Baz, the same way you don't have to justify all the women you sleep with."

"But Roddick?"

I nodded and shoved him aside so I could put my bag down. "Who else? Would it be better if it were one of the prospects?" The dark look that crossed his face told me he didn't think it would. "I've been in love with Roddick since I was a kid, but you wouldn't know that because you weren't here." I held up a hand to stop his attempts to justify his actions. It wasn't necessary. "I'm in love with him, but he doesn't know because he doesn't need to, Baz. I meant it when I said I'm leaving Brently, and since he will never leave, it's a moot point."

"Where will you go?"

"Wherever I want. That's the point."

"He's using you," he bit out.

Those words hurt, and I really wished I could hurt him the same way. "Glad you think so highly of me, Baz. Guess I should've let the boys of CAOS run a train on me a long time ago, huh?"

"Dammit, Cherie!"

"No, Baz, you don't have the right! You and your fuckin' goons cost me every damn date I was ever asked on my whole life! And now that I've chosen a man, even a temporary one, that's not good enough either. Well, that's too damn bad!" I yanked the car door open and growled when he tried to stop me.

"Cherie, please."

"Back off, Baz." I turned the key in the ignition and peeled out of the parking lot without looking back. I loved my brother, I really did, but right now all I wanted was to be somewhere far away from him and everyone else I knew. Since that wasn't an option, I decided to close myself up in my house and indulge in the booze on top of my fridge.

After one Jack and cola, I got an idea and signed up for several nationwide nursing agencies. I might not know where I was going, but maybe I needed an adventure for a year or so until I decided. Yeah, that sounded like a good way to choose my next home.

After that, I spent the night knocking back drinks and preparing myself to say goodbye to the town I'd been born in, raised in, and abandoned in so many years ago. Now, I could also remember it as the place where I fell in love.

***

Roddick

Everything had been set up for my Sunday morning meeting with Lazarus, but still, I had a bad feeling about it. He'd sent a late night text message changing the location, and I let Brockton and Mick know before turning back to Cherie and falling into a dreamless sleep. Now though, waiting by the back door of a Mexican supermarket that had long since gone out of business, I had a feeling nothing was right about any of this. I was just glad Mick and a few guys were nearby. Listening.

When Lazarus showed up with—holy fuck—Salvador Maldonado, Governor of the state of Chihuahua, I knew my instincts were right. The real fucking *el jefe* walked and looked every inch the slick politician he was in a black suit, cowboy boots and a fucking bolero tie. "Glad to finally meet you," he said, wearing that slick Vaseline smile as he shook my hand.

"I wish I could say the same, but I didn't even know you existed," I told him and shook his hand.

Maldonado laughed and shook his head. "Lazarus is the perfect cartel leader, no? He has that crazy eyed thing perfected to scare the boys and keep them in line." He tapped his head. "You know they fear him even though he is a homo, that's a special kind of crazy."

I stared at this crazy motherfucker, talking to me about Lazarus like he wasn't even standing there. Meanwhile, my fucking head was spinning. I expected a Sheriff or maybe a mayor, not the goddamn governor. Lazarus was a puppet. An effective, maniacal puppet, but a puppet just the same. "Well, the man is good at his job."

"And he's soft on you. I'm here to make sure he's not too soft," he said pointedly.

I ignored him. "So are we doing this or will brunch be delivered soon?"

Maldonado laughed and handed me the drugs, leaving Lazarus to take the money as though him not touching it somehow exempted him from the transaction. Asshole. "You are a straight shooter, Roddick. Let's keep it that way, and we will have no problems."

"The same, Maldonado." Surprise flashed in his eyes, but instead of commenting, he turned and left us with nothing more than the sound of his boots on the cracked pavement. Moments later I turned the other way and left, jumping on my bike and headed for Brently with Mick and Torch flanking me after one block. Baz and Cash stayed behind in a truck to see what they had on the tech side of things. We hauled ass over the border, not stopping until we rolled inside the clubhouse storage building on our bikes.

Twenty minutes later, Cash and Baz showed up, and from the look in his eyes, I knew Baz was fired up. "What the fuck is going on? That was the shadiest shit I've ever seen, so start talking. Now!"

He was in my face, but I didn't let my irritation show. "Everything will become clear soon, Baz. You don't know about it because you weren't here," I reminded him with a pointed expression. "Ask Mick. He won't give you details, but he'll tell you it's all legit since your president's word isn't enough."

RODDICK

Baz pushed me again, spitting fire. "If Cherie wasn't in love with you, I would bash your fucking face in right now!" I stood my ground, shoulders squared, and straightened to my full height.

"Same goes," I said quietly, lethally serious.

Torch stepped in between us wearing a creepy ass smile and rubbing his bald head. "You want to scrap Baz, I'm in!"

Baz stared and a moment later the tension fled the room thanks to Torch. "You crazy motherfucker," he laughed, "I may be crazy, but not that damn crazy." Torch let out a howl and wrapped an arm around Baz's shoulders, and just like that, things were cool again. Mostly.

"Now, do you want to show us what you and Cash found or keep shooting daggers my way?"

Cash grinned and opened a heavy duty looking laptop. "Hell yeah, we got the suit and the whack job shaking hands, hugging and laughing. But the best part of all you have to see for yourself."

We crowded around Baz and Cash, eyes glued to the computer screen as Lazarus and Maldonado shook hands. They spoke in rapid fire Spanish and then Lazarus handed him three stacks of the cash I'd placed in Lazarus' hand. "Holy shit!" Mick was the first to break the deafening silence.

"Who's that?" Torch asked.

"That is our cash in the bank," I told him and asked for a copy of the footage. "Store this someplace safe and keep several copies."

"You got it," Cash said, fingers flying over the keyboard while Baz said something about cloud storage, whatever the hell that was.

A few hours later we all dispersed, heading home or into the clubhouse for a few hours with the *pass-arounds*. I made my way home where Cherie was hopefully waiting, and called Brockton on my way. "Stop by as soon as you can."

Chapter Eight

Cherie

It was official. I just got word from Darla that my debt to the hospital had been officially paid off. It took just half the time it was expected to, she pointed out, and reminded me just how valuable I was to the team. I knew she appreciated my hard work and willingness to work extra shifts, but I also knew they'd replace me within two weeks once I was gone.

And now I was free to leave Brently whenever I wanted. Free to leave Roddick too, which was the only thing that gave me pause. Not that I would change my plans and stay in town for him, but now that things were *official,* a dull ache began almost immediately in my chest. The man was imprinted all over my heart, my mind and my body. I couldn't stop thinking about him, couldn't stop myself from wanting him. Worst of all, I couldn't stop imagining a future with him away from Brently.

It was wishful thinking at its best, and I felt utterly disgusted with myself. Still feeling that way when I got home, I hoped a shower would at least wash some of it away, or maybe rinse away the hope swelling in my heart. But it didn't. The one thing that did help was a letter from a hospital in Saskatchewan. They were in need of a well-rounded nurse and apparently that was me, thanks to the headhunting service I signed up with a while back. *One month.* They wanted me there in one month.

I smiled and wiped away the sad tears that had overcome me. It was official. I was leaving Brently. Of course, I needed to see the man who held my heart, maybe to share the good news and maybe to see if I could let him go once and for all.

Can I see you tonight? I texted him wearing a big, goofy grin. He called, and I picked up with an even bigger grin. "Hey."

"I'm on my way home now. Meet me there."

"Okay." I disconnected the call and quickly dressed, taking time to fix my hair and makeup since

RODDICK

I'd probably be spending the night. At that thought, I packed up a few essentials in a bag and then I was ready to go. I started my car and sat there wondering what would happen if I told Roddick I loved him. I wanted him to know I felt that deeply for him, but would it be fair to burden him with my feelings and then up and leave? Would he feel compelled to say it back or make me stay? No answers came so I put the car in gear and made my way to Roddick's bungalow, smiling as I parked on the street.

I'd miss seeing this house regularly. There was something about it, about the neighborhood that always brought a smile to my face. These kids would have a childhood I never had. They could play on the street without worrying about gunshots or rival gangs. They would grow up and date without anything but the usual hardships of dating. I envied them, but I also felt happy for them. "What in the world?" I picked up the phone and dialed Roddick again.

"Can't wait to see me, huh?"

I smiled but my attention was riveted on the overgrown shrubs shielding most of the back yard. "Do you have a redheaded girlfriend, wife, or sister I need to know about? Because she's creeping around your house like a stalker. Or a burglar."

The line was silent for so long I thought maybe he hung up on me. "Stay in the car, Cherie, I'll be there as fast as I can." The line went dead, and I stared at my phone for a long time.

I knew something was going on because something was always going on with CAOS, but now, worry settled in a ball deep in my gut. The woman clearly didn't know Roddick well if she thought there would be an easy way inside his home. I stayed in the driver's seat wondering what the hell was going on when I lost sight of the redhead.

A knock sounded on the window, and I nearly jumped out of my skin. But then I saw the woman tapped on my window with a black gun, a nine millimeter. "Come on out."

RODDICK

"No thanks," I told her, sliding my phone in the pocket of my dress and dialed Roddick again. "I'm good here."

She grinned but it was more of a snarl. "It wasn't a question, sweetheart. Get the fuck out of the car."

"If you insist," I told her and pushed out of the car. "What do you want, Ms.?"

"My name isn't important and neither is yours. Just open the front door, and we won't have any problems." Wide green eyes darted back and forth, but despite the crazed look in her eyes, she held herself like a cop.

Just what I needed, a fucking psycho with a gun. "I can't open the fucking door, lady, why the hell do you think I was waiting in my car?"

She groaned and pushed me up the steps, tapping her foot impatiently in front of the door. "You're way prettier than I thought a biker's old lady would be."

"Thanks," I said with a bitter laugh, "but I'm not his old lady. Just a piece of ass. Thanks for ruining my last night with him, by the way. I really appreciate *that*." This woman was off her rocker, but I'd dealt with worse in the ER.

"Nope, try again, blondie. I know you've been seeing each other, staying the night and all. Now be cool and let me in and you won't get hurt." She pushed me until the doorknob pressed into my stomach. "I need you to make sure your boyfriend doesn't do anything stupid."

I laughed at that and she stepped back, gun still pointed at the ground. "If you think I have any sway over him, you're dead ass wrong and you might as well give up now."

"In that case, your night is about to get really bad."

***

Roddick

"I'm going to kill that fucking bitch!" My heart pounded in my throat as I listened to Agent Molly fucking Johnson hold a gun on Cherie. I was happy I left my bike at the clubhouse because there was something satisfying as fuck about pressing the pedal to the metal.

"Slow down," Brockton urged from the passenger seat. "You won't be much good to your girl if you're dead." The man had stopped by Mick's service station to pass me a message. Lazarus had been found dead two hours ago, half of his body on the American side and half on the Mexican side. Brockton thought the task force had a mole or I did.

"I guess now we have our answer." I cut a quick glance at Brockton who looked angry and worried, his gaze focused on the road ahead.

The streets of Brently were quiet, and after a few hairpin turns on quiet residential streets, I brought the car to a screeching halt at the corner. "I'll go through the front since she's expecting me. There's a key buried at the bottom of the bird feeder back there."

Brockton grinned. "Making sure your fortress is impenetrable?"

"What's the matter, Captain America, afraid of a little bird seed?"

"Fuck off," he laughed and jumped out. "Be careful."

"Be more worried about your partner," I told him and sped off, slamming on the brakes in my driveway. I took two beats before climbing from the car and up the steps. I couldn't let this bitch get me too riled up, and I'd be damned if I let her hurt Cherie. Feeling as calm as I could, I stepped inside the house and found Molly in my recliner and Cherie sitting on the other side of the room facing her, eyes glued to the gun in Molly's hand. "Cherie, you okay?" She nodded, and I turned to the woman I itched to kill. "Molly, to what do I owe the displeasure of this visit?" I gave her a charming, sickly sweet smile which she didn't bother to return.

"You have some footage I need."

I blinked as her words registered because I'd been expecting something else. Hell, anything else. "Footage?"

RODDICK

That sent the tiny witch into a rage. "Don't fucking play dumb with me!" She waved the gun around carelessly, eyes wild, movements jerky. "Just give me everything you have, photos and video, of Lazarus and the Governor and I'll walk out of here. You and your girlfriend—sorry, your ol' lady—get to live."

I barked out a laugh. "You can't expect me to believe that shit, Pollyanna. You're itching to pull that trigger," I told her, taking a few casual steps to my left to shield Cherie from any bullets that might fly.

"I can still pull the trigger," she said, still waving the gun. "Say that you pulled a gun on me and I had to drop you, then the blonde when she tried to avenge you. It's all covered," she smiled that famous tweaker smile that was half overexcited six-year-old and half crazed murderer.

"Sounds like a good plan. Except for one thing."

"Except nothing, goddammit!"

I smiled and shoved my hands in my pockets. "Except Brockton already has the footage."

"No!"

"'Fraid so. And there's the matter of Lazarus' fail safe in case of his death." Her eyes went wide telling me that she had something to do with that. "He was a clever little fucker, and he knew one day that slimy politician would turn on him."

"What does that mean?"

"It means while you're over here trying to scare my woman half to death, your world has been blown the fuck up. *Agent*."

"Shit! Shit, shit, shit, shit!" She was losing it, pacing back and forth and waving that fucking gun like it was a battle flag. She stopped and glared at me, then Cherie and back at me with a gleam in her crazed eyes. "Then I guess I don't need either of you." She raised the gun, and I took that final step in front of Cherie, pulling my hands from my pocket.

"Maybe not. Just make sure you save a bullet for yourself because you're going to want to kill yourself real soon. Cops don't last long in prison."

"Nah, that idiot Brockton is back at the office and this little shit can town is close enough to the border that I'll be gone before he realizes what happened." Her lips pursed and her brows dipped when she couldn't see Cherie. "Move your ass, biker boy."

"Can't do that, Pollyanna. Your beef is with me."

"But it'll hurt you so much more if I shoot her first." She grinned like the fucking psychopath she was.

"You should be worried about your own pain," I told her, stiffening when I felt Cherie's hand wrap around the gun tucked in the back of my pants.

"Come on out, blondie, or your boyfriend gets it."

I felt the cool steel on my hand and grasped it, breathing a little easier until Cherie stepped in front of me, arms crossed, a look of defiance on her face. "There's just one hitch in your plan," she said, her voice soft and calm despite the pulse beating at the base of her neck.

"I'm sure you're gonna tell me, Nightingale?"

Cherie nodded. "I'm sure there are cartel members at your home, airports, train and bus stations, and sitting at the border waiting to tie up one final loose end. You."

I was proud of my girl for staying cool during this shit, but she'd just pissed Molly off, and the gun was raised and aimed again. "You little whore!" Then she squeezed the trigger, and Cherie spun around before dropping to the floor at the same time two more bullets thundered in the room, and Molly fell where she stood.

Brockton entered through the kitchen and went straight to Molly, kicking her gun away. "She'll live," he said with disgust and dropped to his knees to be sure. I could hardly focus on his words or that bitch. I was too concerned with my woman.

RODDICK

"Cherie, baby. Are you okay?" I turned her, searching for any signs of blood, patting her body gently for wounds when she began to groan.

"That fucking hurt, and it was just a graze." She turned her shoulder to show the gash in her skin where the bullet flew by. "Shit, not a graze!" She glanced over at Molly and quickly crawled to her on one arm, grabbing a throw blanket to staunch the bleeding at her neck.

I sat amazed by the woman I saw. This bitch had shot her yet, there she was, kneeling over her body in an effort to save her life. Her skin was pale though and her movements were jerky, a sure sign of shock, but she held the wound until two burly paramedics came in and took over. She rattled off the wounds she spotted and stepped back, blood covering her pretty little dress. "Did you wear that just for me?"

She looked down, finally seeing the blood covering her hands, her clothes. Then the tears came and absolutely fucking gutted me. I went to her and wrapped her in my arm. "Oh, honey, you did damn good. I'm proud of you."

"We need to go. Now," Brockton said and guided us to a standard issue government SUV, idling at the curb.

Cherie clutched my hand tight and I held her close, letting her cry the whole way to the task force headquarters.

Chapter Nine

Cherie

"Y-you mean that, *Señorita*?" Bonnie gripped my hand, her dark eyes full of hope and gratitude.

"I do. Lazarus is dead, and the governor is in prison. Would you like to call your family now?"

She shook her head, and I was ready to argue until she shocked the hell out of me. "I already called them, Cherie. They want me to come home."

I smiled down at her, glad to hear this wouldn't completely tear her life apart. "If you help the police, they will help you get home." I gave her the details, and she promised to call as soon as she was discharged later that day. "Good luck, Bonnie."

"You, too. Thank you, angel."

I smiled and left the hospital for the last time. Outside I turned toward the sun, letting the heat heal me. A week had passed since I'd been shot in Roddick's home, and I spent that time packing up my life in preparation for my move. To Canada. That still felt weird to say, but I'd called and accepted the job as soon as one of my colleagues stitched me up, so I had three weeks to make it to some small town in Saskatchewan.

"You gonna let the sun molest you all day or get your ass in gear?"

I rolled my eyes at Baz, giving him an indulgent smile. "Might be the last molesting I get for a while."

"Aww, come on, Cher. I never need to hear that shit again," he groaned and pushed open the passenger door. "Get in."

"Where are we going?"

"It's a surprise," he said and hit the gas the moment my seatbelt clicked.

It didn't take much time to realize where he was taking me. The clubhouse. "Baz, come on, I'm not in the mood." I was less than not in the mood. For the past week, I'd had nightmares every time I closed my eyes, anxiety from all the law enforcement grilling and despite the graze, I was also in constant pain. Though maybe that was heartache.

"In the mood to hang out with people you've known your entire life?" he asked angrily.

"Dammit, Baz, don't put words in my mouth!" I took in several deep breaths to slow down my heart. "I don't want to be in a roomful of people carrying guns after...everything. You ever think of that?"

He quickly pulled over and gathered me in his arms. "Shit no, sis, I didn't think of that. I'm sorry." His warm arms held me close while he softly swore under his breath. "You have to say goodbye, Cher, these guys have known you all your life."

I nodded against his chest because he was right. In two days, I'd put Brently in my rearview mirror, and chances were good I might never see many of them again. "I'll go," I sighed, chuckling when he put the car in gear and started driving again. "I'm gonna miss you, Baz."

"No you won't because I'm visiting once a month. At least."

"It's a thirty-hour drive, so I doubt that very much," I laughed.

"Small town girls are freaky," he said and wiggled his eyebrows.

"Gross." I smacked his arm as we pulled up in front of the clubhouse. "Is he going to be there?" I hadn't seen Roddick all week, and in a way it helped me get started on living without him, though it hurt like hell that he'd just forgotten about me.

Baz sighed and nodded. "He got back two days ago. Had to go to D.C. and Mexico to give statements and shit."

We entered the bar area of the clubhouse and I paused, took my time looking around. I'd grown up in this place with scantily clad women leaning over every surface to show off their bodies, with gun toting bikers who really were big softies. I learned how to play pool at that table with the scuff mark in front of the center right pocket. I snuck my first drink from a metal card table in the corner when Torch left me unattended. A smile touched the corners of my mouth thinking about those moments. Those years when this place had been the only real home I'd known.

This was the place I grew to love Roddick. Swiping away tears, I turned to the bar and waved at Talon and her little baby and a very pregnant Minx. "Hi, girls. You're both looking good."

Talon and Minx both found their way to Brently though their connection with Magnus, though through very different circumstances. Minx didn't like to discuss it. She'd been kidnapped and pulled into a human trafficking ring. Rumor was they'd finally found her parent's, but she didn't want anything to do with them. Said it was better if they think she's dead. It was a sad notion to consider, but I guessed she was happy here, and that was what mattered.

Talon, on the other hand, only came to Brently because of Magnus' estate. Her father. Unfortunately, she never even knew him. And he was such a good man.

Talon pulled me into a hug, and I pressed a kiss to Megan's sweet head. "I can't believe you're leaving!"

Minx rolled her eyes and gave me a hug. "You're really going out there, living your life. Very cool."

"Thanks. You don't think I'm running away?"

"Hell no! I think you're brave as hell. I wanted to leave, but I went and fell in love." She cast a loving gaze at Cash who'd just come from Church with Mick, Torch, Dagger, Rich and Roddick.

"You probably got the better deal," I told her, hearing the wistfulness in my voice. "Take care of each other," I told them. "I always wished I had friends like you growing up." But all the girls wanted to get close to Baz or one of the other guys, not me.

"Good luck out there!"

"How's it going?"

RODDICK

I turned and gave Baz my best attempt at a smile. "Fine. What's going on?"

He nodded to where Roddick stood. "Talk to him, he might surprise you."

"I doubt that." But he was already making his way over so I didn't really have a choice. "Hi."

"Hey." He sounded nervous, unsure. I'd never seen or heard Roddick look anything less than perfectly capable and fully in charge. "Walk with me?"

I took his hand and let him guide me around the back and up the fire ladder on the side of the main building. When we reached the top, I gasped. "It's amazing up here!" A rooftop oasis with plants and flowers dotting the perimeter, comfortable sofas and chairs, tables topped with candles and a giant ashtray. Off to the side was a grill along with a picnic table. "Did you do this?"

"Been working on it all year." His gaze was filled with longing. "I've missed you."

"I've been where I always am, Roddick. You couldn't have missed me that much." I knew it wasn't fair as soon as I said it. "Sorry."

"It's okay, you're right. I should have called, but I needed to make sure everything was taken care of before I came back to you, Cherie."

Words I always wanted to hear. "What's going on, Roddick?"

He guided me to the gray cushioned sofa and held my hands in his before taking a long breath. Then he started talking. And talking. About the task force, the drugs, the cartel and taking down the governor of Chihuahua. Everything. "I'm not the Prez anymore."

My eyes went wide and I grabbed his face. "Roddick, no!" No one ever left CAOS of their own free will. "You're...?" I couldn't even voice it, it was just too awful to think about.

He smiled and pressed a kiss to the center of my palm. "I'm glad to see you're still worried about me, but you don't need to be. I'm not out of CAOS, not officially, but I'm no longer an active member. In fact, I'm leaving California altogether."

There was so much to dissect about just a few short sentences that I had no clue where to start processing. I tried to focus on one thing, just one thing, and finally, it came into focus. "Where are you going?"

He shrugged. "I'm not sure yet. This chick I'm in love with just got a job and she's moving to some place called Saka. . .Sasketcha. . . oh, fuck, Canada, so I thought I'd check that out."

It took a moment, but as soon as I felt a tear slide down my cheek I knew I'd heard right. My lips trembled. "Y-you mean that? You're in love with me?"

He nodded, smiling in bemusement. "You didn't know?"

"Don't I seem shocked enough?" I couldn't believe it. This big handsome man was in love with me *and* he wanted to move with me. "Oh, Roddick, I am so in love with you, too. I have been since...well, forever."

He smiled as I slid closer, scooping me up and onto his lap. "It feels like I've been in love with you forever, too. Does that make me a dirty old man?"

I shook my head with a smile. "Fuck yeah, baby. It makes you *my* dirty old man."

Then he pressed his mouth to mine in a smoldering kiss that quickly caught fire. His lips felt strong, soft, insistent as they coaxed mine open to let his tongue slide in. It just felt right. Amazing. Perfect. His hands were warm against my cool skin, so big as they cupped my ass and brought me closer. His tongue delved deeper and I moaned, letting my body relax into his. I was finally...letting go. Roddick was the first to pull back and dotted my neck and jaw with kisses. "That sounds like perfection to me, Cherie."

"Me too." I smiled at him, unable to stop the silly happy grin that spread across my face.

"So...Canada?"

RODDICK

I nodded and took another taste of his lips. "Canada."

KB Winters

Epilogue

Roddick *~Two years later*

Holding my wife's naked body in my hands while I thrust into her was the best damn part of the cold ass days and arctic nights here in Canada. Our new home was at least twice as big as the apartment we lived in our first year in town. Now we had a house. A home. With a fireplace in the bedroom, which came in pretty handy because Cherie loved making love by a roaring fire. "Someone's feeling frisky today."

She laughed and tightened her legs around my waist, licking the sweat from my neck in one naughty swipe. "I can't help it. I think it's the storm, so dangerous and wicked."

"Or maybe," I kissed one side of her neck and then the other, "it's the pregnancy hormones." I dotted kisses down her body until I came to the small swell of her belly where our baby grew inside.

She laughed and pulled me up for another kiss. "I'm only four and a half months, I think that's too soon for the horniness stage."

"You mean this is just you and there's more to come...later?"

She smacked my ass and kissed my mouth. "You're insatiable! That's how I got like this in the first place."

Yeah, we'd spent the first few months in our tiny apartment lost in each other. Losing ourselves in the passion of our love. She worked during the day, and I made us a home. "Have you told your brother about the baby yet?"

"No. I wanted to make sure we were out of the woods first." She nibbled her bottom lip which she only did when she was nervous.

"What is it, darlin'?"

"Nothing. I just...I'm nervous."

"Baz is cool with this. Remember the wedding?" He'd gotten us both rip roaring drunk in Niagara

Falls and we had the time of our lives, and we had plenty of photos to prove it.

"No, not that. About being pregnant and having the baby."

"You're a nurse, Cherie."

"Exactly, I know what can go wrong."

"You'll be fine. I'll be right there with you the whole time."

"How did I get so lucky, Roddick? I love you."

I kissed her for all I was worth and we came together fast and hard, passionate before we both collapsed on the bed with a gasping laugh. "You didn't get lucky, Cherie, I did. Never forget that." I wiped her tears and pulled her close.

"I won't because you are the best husband in the world."

"You have a way of making me feel like a superhero, baby." I kissed her again and slid from the bed. "I have a surprise for you. Put this on." I tossed her a robe and waited by the door.

"What are you up to, Rod?"

"You'll see." I pulled her along to the room we settled on for the nursery and pushed open the door.

"Oh my God, Roddick! This is. . .amazing." Awe filled her voice and she looked up at me with tears in her eyes, and I really did feel like a fucking superhero.

"I'm glad you like it, babe." Woodworking was my new gig, my new passion. I had a shop out back where I made tables, rocking chairs, statutes and pretty much anything else people in North America were willing to buy at my prices. Apparently, high-quality hand-crafted wood was in high demand. "I have a rocker in the works so you can sit right here and nurse our baby."

She cupped my jaw so tenderly, the way she often did when her emotions were high. "Are you sure this is what you want, Roddick? You've transformed into a sexy lumberjack but..."

RODDICK

I sighed because she asked ever so often, and I loved her for it. "Cherie, I am right where I want to be. With you, my beautiful wife." CAOS was doing fine, thriving even in Brently and beyond. They'd given us half of the ten million dollar reward money from the FBI, but we insisted they kept the money from the other agencies who'd piled charges on Maldonado and about a dozen other Mexican Devils, Molly Johnson, and a few other Mexican politicians. It was a nice nest egg for us and much appreciated.

"I'm glad because I love our life here, even if I do miss Baz. And Torch."

"We'll visit once the baby is born. I miss them, too."

"If we can," she said. We'd been advised by Brockton to stay out of the U.S. until everyone had been tried and convicted in all jurisdictions.

"If we can't then we'll have a big ass party up here. Can you imagine them in this cold?"

We made our way back to our bedroom, and Cherie snuggled closer to me as we sat in front of the fire. "I can't but I would love to!"

"Then let's make it happen. When the baby gets here."

"Babies," she clarified and looked up at me with tears shimmering in her eyes. "We're having *babies,* Roddick."

"Babies? Twins?" She nodded and I stood, slipping on my long johns and jeans. "Twins?"

"Yes! Where are you going? Are you upset about this?"

I frowned up at her. "Upset? Hell no, I'm excited!"

"Then where are you going?"

"We need another crib and another rocking chair plus two little armoires—and in the next four months!" She laughed and it was the sweetest damn sound I'd ever heard. I knew I'd spend the rest of my life keeping that look of love on her face and aimed right at me.

~ THE END ~

KB Winters

Acknowledgements

Thank you! I love you all and thank you for making my books a success!! I appreciate each and every one of you.

Thanks to all of my beta readers, street teamers, ARC readers and Facebook fans. Y'all are THE BEST!

And a huge very special thanks to my wonderful PA, Silla. Without you, I'd be a hot mess! With you, I'm a hot mess, but without your keen sense of organization and skills, I'd be a burny fiery inferno of hot mess!! Thank you!

And a very special thanks to my editor, Silla Webb (who sometimes has to work all through the night! See HOT MESS above!) Thank you for making my words make sense.

Copyright © 2017 BookBoyfriends Publishing LLC KB WINTERS

About The Author

KB Winters has an addiction to caffeine, tattoos and hard-bodied alpha males. The men in her books are very sexy, protective and sometimes bossy, her ladies are...well...bossier!

Living in sunny Southern California, the embarrassingly hopeless romantic writes every chance she gets!

You can connect with KB on Facebook (https://www.facebook.com/kbwintersauthor) and Twitter (http://twitter.com/kbwintersauthor)!

Printed in Great Britain
by Amazon